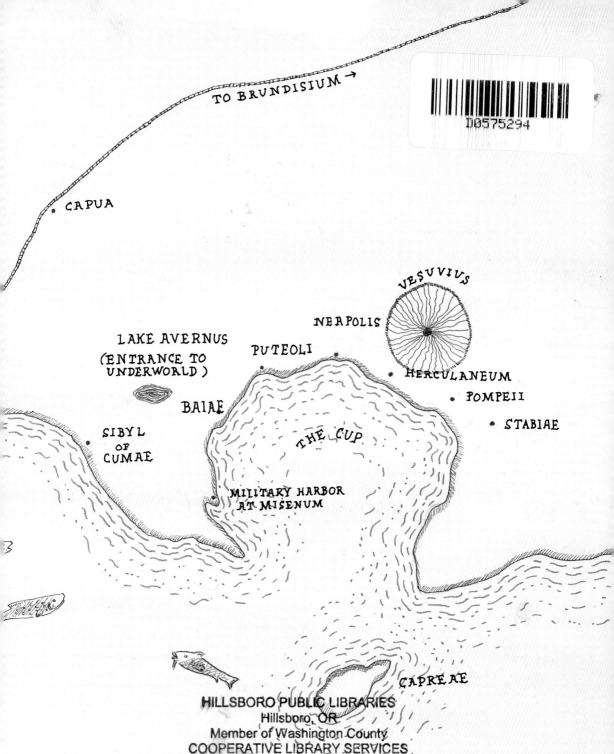

TO BRUNDISIUM →

CAPUA

VESUVIUS

NEAPOLIS

LAKE AVERNUS
(ENTRANCE TO
UNDERWORLD)

PUTEOLI

HERCULANEUM

POMPEII

BAIAE

STABIAE

SIBYL
OF
CUMAE

THE CUP

MILITARY HARBOR
AT MISENUM

CAPREAE

MAUSOLEUM
OF
AUGUSTUS

☀

PINCIAN HILL

VIA FLAMINIA

VIA SALARIA

ARA PACIS
(ALTAR OF PEACE)

SERVIAN WALLS

COLLINE
GATE

VIA NOMENTANA

CAMPUS
MARTIUS

VIA TRIUMPHALIS

QUIRINAL HILL

VOTING
STALLS

PANTHEON

BATHS
OF
AGRIPPA

VIMINAL HILL

VIA TIBURTINA

THEATRE
OF
POMPEY

PORTICUS

SAEPTA

FORUM OF
AUGUSTUS

SUBURA

VIA PRAENESTINA

STABLES
OF
GREENS

CIRCUS
FLAMINIUS

CAPITOLINE

FORUM ROMANUM

ROSTRA

ESQUILINE
HILL

JANICULUM HILL

THEAT
OF
MARCELLUS

TEMPLE
OF JUPITER

PALANTINE

HOUSE OF
AUGUSTUS

VIA SACRA

VIA AURELIA

CIRCUS MAXIMUS

CAELIAN
HILL

NAUMACHIA
OF
AUGUSTUS
(ARTIFICIAL LAKE)

AVENTINE
HILL

CAPENA
GATE

VIA OSTENSE

APPIAN WAY

VIA LATINA

ROME

SPQR
SENATUS PUBLICUS
QUE ROMANUS

MARISSA MOSS

GALEN

MY LIFE IN IMPERIAL ROME

SILVER WHISTLE • HARCOURT, INC.

San Diego   New York   London

AI MIEI RAGAZZI ROMANI

www.HarcourtBooks.com

Silver Whistle is a trademark of Harcourt, Inc.,
registered in the United States of America and/or other jurisdictions.

Library of Congress Cataloging-in-Publication Data
Moss, Marissa.
Galen: my life in imperial Rome/Marissa Moss.
p. cm.—(An ancient world journal; 1)
"Silver Whistle."
Summary: Twelve-year-old Galen describes his life as a slave in Rome under the Emperor Augustus.
Features hand-printed text, drawings, and marginal notes.
1. Rome—History—Augustus, 30 B.C.–14 A.D.—Juvenile Fiction.
[1. Rome—History—Augustus, 30 B.C.–14 A.D.—Fiction.
2. Slaves—Fiction. 3. Diaries—Fiction.] I. Title.
PZ7.M8535Gal 2002
[Fic]—dc21   2001039890
ISBN 0-15-216535-5

3651 9667 11/07

CEGHFD

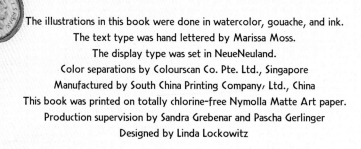

The illustrations in this book were done in watercolor, gouache, and ink.
The text type was hand lettered by Marissa Moss.
The display type was set in NeueNeuland.
Color separations by Colourscan Co. Pte. Ltd., Singapore
Manufactured by South China Printing Company, Ltd., China
This book was printed on totally chlorine-free Nymolla Matte Art paper.
Production supervision by Sandra Grebenar and Pascha Gerlinger
Designed by Linda Lockowitz

I AM NOT A WRITER BUT A PAINTER, LIKE MY FATHER AND MY GRANDFATHER AND MY GRANDFATHER'S FATHER. I PICK UP MY PEN TO SKETCH WORDS RATHER THAN PICTURES BECAUSE OF AN AMAZING DISCOVERY I HAVE MADE. I WAS REACHING FOR A SCROLL TO READ WHEN I NOTICED LODGED BEHIND IT, AGAINST THE BACK WALL OF THE SHELF, ANOTHER SCROLL. I PRIED IT OUT AND REALIZED I WAS HOLDING A WORK I'D NEVER SEEN BEFORE.

IT WAS NOT POETRY, HISTORY, OR AN ARGUMENT MADE BEFORE THE LAW COURTS BUT SOMETHING MUCH MORE PRECIOUS — THE LIFE OF MY GRANDFATHER WRITTEN WHEN HE WAS A BOY OF TWELVE, ONLY FOUR YEARS YOUNGER THAN ME, COMPLETE WITH HIS OWN ILLUSTRATIONS. I NEVER MET MY GRANDFATHER WHO DIED BEFORE I WAS BORN, BUT READING HIS WORDS I NOW FEEL I KNOW HIM VERY WELL.

MY GRANDFATHER WAS A SLAVE NAMED GALEN. HE WAS FORTUNATE ENOUGH TO HAVE LIVED UNDER (AND EVEN WITH!) THAT GREATEST OF EMPERORS, AUGUSTUS, NOW DEIFIED AS A GOD. AND RIGHTLY SO, AS HE WAS WISE, GOOD, AND JUST, HIS VIRTUES ALL THE MORE GOLDEN AS THE EMPERORS AFTER HIM

HAVE BEEN VICIOUS AND CRUEL. TIBERIUS, HIS STEPSON, SUCCEEDED HIM, A MAN DESCRIBED BY HIS OWN TUTOR AS A MIXTURE OF MUD AND BLOOD. UNFORTUNATELY, MORE BLOOD THAN MUD — SUSPICIOUS OF ALL, SMELLING CONSPIRACY EVERYWHERE. THOSE HE SUSPECTED, WOMEN AND CHILDREN AS WELL AS MEN, WERE PULLED BY HOOKS DOWN THE STAIRS OF MOURNING AND THROWN INTO THE TIBER AS FOOD FOR THE FISHES. WHEN HE DIED, NO ONE SORROWED. RUMOR HAS IT THAT HE WAS FED POISON OR SMOTHERED UNDER A PILLOW, BUT I THINK THE OLD GOAT DIED NATURALLY — HE WAS SEVENTY-SEVEN YEARS OLD AFTER ALL.

AFTER TIBERIUS CAME HIS GREAT-NEPHEW, CALIGULA, WHO BEGAN HIS BLOODY REIGN BY MURDERING HIS OWN MOTHER AND ENDED IT FOUR SHORT YEARS LATER KILLED BY HIS OWN PRAETORIAN GUARD.

THE MAN WAS INSANE, MADE MAD WITH POWER. HE DRESSED HIS FAVORITE RACEHORSE IN IMPERIAL PURPLE AND MADE HIM A SENATOR. I SUPPOSE AT LEAST THE ANIMAL HAD HORSE SENSE!

CALIGULA WAS FOLLOWED BY HIS UNCLE, CLAUDIUS, THE HALF-WIT. HE, TOO, WAS KILLED, FED POISONED MUSHROOMS BY HIS WIFE, AGRIPPINA, SO THAT HER OWN SON, NERO, COULD RULE ROME. AND RULE HE NOW DOES.

I CANNOT COMPLAIN TOO MUCH ABOUT NERO FOR HE PAYS ME VERY WELL TO PAINT THE WALLS OF HIS GOLDEN PALACE. IT IS AS WONDROUS AS THEY SAY. ENORMOUS, YES, WITH A LARGE ARTIFICIAL LAKE IN ITS PARK AND A COLOSSAL STATUE OF NERO CXX FEET TALL.

ONE RUMOR HAS IT THAT NERO SANG WHILE THE GREAT FIRE RAGED, SO UNCONCERNED WAS HE. OTHERS SAY HE SET THE FIRE HIMSELF TO CLEAR ROOM FOR HIS PALACE AND GARDENS. I DON'T KNOW IF EITHER IS TRUE, BUT FOR CERTAIN, HE'S HAPPY TO HAVE SO MANY SHODDY TENEMENTS GONE.

I AM NO HAPPIER ABOUT THE FIRE THAT DEVOURED MUCH OF ROME THAN ANYONE ELSE. MY OWN HOME WAS SPARED THOUGH A THIRD OF THE CITY LAY IN ASHES. I SHUDDER TO SEE THE BLAME FOR THE CALAMITY HEAPED ON A STRANGE RELIGIOUS SECT.

THOSE POOR PEOPLE WHO CALL THEMSELVES CHRISTIANS AFTER THEIR GOD, THE CHRIST, DO NOT SEEM LIKE EVIL THREATS. I STAY AT HOME WHEN THEY ARE BURNED ALIVE OR THROWN TO THE BEASTS.

IN THE PALACE THE CEILING OF THE DOMED DINING ROOM REVOLVES, MAKING THE STARS PAINTED ON IT WHEEL OVERHEAD, WHILE PERFUME SPRAYS OUT FROM PIPES IN THE WALLS. WHAT LUXURY!

BUT I WRITE TOO MUCH ABOUT MYSELF. MY INTENT WAS TO INTRODUCE MY GRANDFATHER AND HIS TIMES, FOR I HAVE DECIDED TO COPY HIS PAPYRUS SCROLL ONTO PARCHMENT AND HAVE IT BOUND INTO A CODEX, OR BOOK, TO MAKE IT EASIER TO READ. I WILL COPY BOTH HIS WORDS AND PICTURES, BUT TO BEGIN THIS, I WILL USE THE SELF-PORTRAIT HE PAINTED SO I CAN SEE HIS EYES MEET MINE.

GAIUS OCTAVIANUS ZOSIMUS
DCCCXX AB URBE CONDITA, IDES OF JULIUS

I WAS NOT BORN A SLAVE, BUT ON A TRIP ACROSS THE PIRAEUS, OUR BOAT WAS CAPTURED BY PIRATES. WARS AND PIRACY MAKE MANY SLAVES.

I AM CALLED GALEN AND AM TWELVE YEARS OLD IN THE YEAR DCCLII AB URBE CONDITA, LIVING IN THE CENTER OF THE WORLD, ROME. THERE, THAT'S A PLAIN ENOUGH START AND NOT AS HARD AS I THOUGHT IT WOULD BE.

I KNOW I'M YOUNG TO BE WRITING DOWN MY LIFE, BUT MY MASTER, THE EMPEROR AUGUSTUS, HAS ENCOURAGED ME. HE IS WRITING HIS OWN LIFE, MUCH MORE INTERESTING THAN MINE, OF COURSE, AND SAYS I SHOULD DO THE SAME. "NOT BECAUSE YOU HAVE DONE GREAT THINGS," HE SAYS, "BUT TO MOLD YOUR MIND SO YOU WILL DO GREAT THINGS. WRITING HELPS CREATE A MORAL WORLD. YOU HAVE ONLY TO READ VIRGIL TO RECOGNIZE THE POWER OF WORDS."

THEN HE QUOTES HIS OTHER FAVORITE POET, HORACE, SAYING, "BE BRIEF," AND "MORE OUGHT TO BE SCRATCHED OUT THAN LEFT." WRITING LESS SOUNDS EASY, BUT DRAWING COMES MORE NATURALLY TO ME, SO THIS PAPYRUS CAN ALSO SERVE AS A SKETCHBOOK. I WANT TO WRITE WELL TO PLEASE AUGUSTUS, BUT I MUST DRAW WELL TO SERVE MY FATHER, TO BECOME A FINE PAINTER LIKE HE IS.

SHOULD I DESCRIBE MYSELF OR SET THE STAGE, DESCRIBING LIFE HERE IN THE PALACE? I TAKE UP FEW WORDS - I AM SLIGHT AND DARK WITH A CLEAR VOICE GOOD FOR READING ALOUD TO DINNER GUESTS. AGRIPPA POSTUMUS, AUGUSTUS' GRANDSON WHO IS BEING RAISED HERE, IS TWO YEARS YOUNGER THAN ME, AND WE USED TO STUDY TOGETHER. BUT HE HATES BOOKS, HATES MY LIKING THEM AND READING THEM WELL, AND, MOST OF ALL, HATES ME.

AGRIPPA POSTUMUS IS THE YOUNGEST CHILD OF JULIA, AUGUSTUS' DAUGHTER, AND AGRIPPA, HIS GENERAL. THE GENERAL DIED BEFORE HIS SON'S BIRTH. THAT'S WHY THE SON IS CALLED POSTUMUS.

BUT I DON'T WANT TO WRITE ABOUT AGRIPPA, THE BULLY WHO SOURS MY DAYS, NOT YET. I WANT TO WRITE ABOUT THE BEGINNING. NOT WHEN I WAS BORN, BUT OF THE DAY FIVE YEARS AGO WHEN I FIRST SAW THE EMPEROR.

NOW TO SET THE SCENE. MY FATHER IS FAMOUS FOR THE BEAUTY OF HIS ART. WHEN HE WAS BROUGHT TO THE SLAVE MARKET IN NEAPOLIS, HE FETCHED A HIGH PRICE AND WAS BOUGHT BY VEDIUS POLLIO.

SLAVES WEAR IRON OR BRONZE SIGNS AROUND THEIR NECKS TELLING THEIR AGES AND QUALITIES. THEIR FEET ARE MARKED WITH CHALK.

GREEK SLAVES LIKE US ARE USUALLY SKILLED AND VALUABLE, UNLIKE THE POOR THRACIANS OR GAULS, WHO OFTEN END UP IN THE MINES OR ROWING PRIVATE SHIPS. (THOSE IN THE ROMAN ARMY CANNOT BE SLAVES, BUT MUST BE FREE MEN.) FATHER ASSURED US HE WOULD BE FREED EVENTUALLY AND COULD THEN BUY ME AND MY BROTHER. BUT HOW LONG WOULD THAT TAKE?

VEDIUS POLLIO WAS BORN A FREEDMAN HIMSELF, MEANING HIS OWN FATHER HAD BEEN A SLAVE, BUT THAT MADE HIM NO KINDER A MASTER. HE HAD RISEN IN STATUS AND WEALTH TO REACH THE EQUESTRIAN ORDER, JUST SHY OF BECOMING A SENATOR, THE HIGHEST LEVEL OF ALL. AS AN EQUESTRIAN HE'D BEEN GRANTED THE GOVERNORSHIP OF A PROVINCE AND RETURNED TO ROME EVEN RICHER, AS MOST GOVERNORS DO, HAVING ROBBED THE PROVINCE BLIND. LIKE MANY WEALTHY ROMANS, HE HAD A MANSION IN ROME AND A LARGE VILLA IN BAIAE NEAR NEAPOLIS. THE VILLA WAS THE REASON HE BOUGHT MY FATHER (AND US, OF COURSE, ALONG WITH HIM).

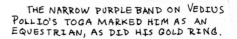

THE NARROW PURPLE BAND ON VEDIUS POLLIO'S TOGA MARKED HIM AS AN EQUESTRIAN, AS DID HIS GOLD RING.

BAIAE IS A RESORT TOWN, WITH A SPA OF HEALING WATERS AND NEARBY LAKE LUCRINUS TO BOAT IN. BUT IT IS ALSO AN OLD GREEK SETTLEMENT, AND PEOPLE THERE AROUND THE CUP (AS THE BAY IS CALLED) SPEAK GREEK MORE OFTEN THAN LATIN. THE ANCIENT SIBYL IS NEARBY IN CUMAE, AS IS THE ENTRANCE TO THE UNDERWORLD. IT IS A PLACE OF DEEP MYSTERY AS WELL AS LIGHT PLEASURE.

VEDIUS POLLIO WANTED TO OUTDO HIS NEIGHBORS IN LUXURY. (SUCH OSTENTATION IS FROWNED UPON IN ROME, SO IT THRIVES HERE.) MY FATHER WAS CHARGED WITH PAINTING THE VILLA AS ELABORATELY AS POSSIBLE. I WAS TOO YOUNG THEN TO PAINT WITH HIM AS I DO NOW, BUT I PREPARED THE COLORS, CLEANED THE BRUSHES, AND DID THE FINAL STEP OF SEALING THE PICTURES WITH ENCAUSTIC VARNISH. MY BROTHER, POLYNICES, WHO IS THREE YEARS OLDER THAN ME, COULD HAVE PAINTED SIMPLE THINGS LIKE FRAMES AND LEAVES, BUT HE INHERITED MY MOTHER'S BEAUTY INSTEAD OF MY FATHER'S TALENT. CHARMED BY HIS CURLS AND LUSH EYELASHES, POLLIO CHOSE POLYNICES TO BE HIS CUPBEARER, A GANYMEDE OF SORTS, THOUGH POLLIO WAS NO ZEUS!

THE VILLA'S ATRIUM

OUR LIFE THERE WAS NOT BAD. MY FATHER STILL MOURNED MY MOTHER'S DEATH AND THE REVERSAL OF FORTUNE THAT HAD TURNED HIM FROM FREE MAN TO SLAVE. BUT HE TOOK CONSOLATION IN HIS ART AND IN US, HIS SONS, AND PRAYED TO THE GODS THAT OUR FORTUNES BE RESTORED. PERHAPS THE OLYMPIANS WERE SLEEPING THEN. THEY CERTAINLY DIDN'T HELP US.

INSTEAD THINGS GOT SUDDENLY MUCH, MUCH WORSE.

THE VILLA FACES THE SEA.

IT WAS A CRISP FALL DAY, AND THE SLAVES OF THE VILLA WERE RUNNING AROUND PREPARING FOR A SPECIAL GUEST. MY FATHER HAD FINISHED THE MAIN ROOMS, AND VEDIUS POLLIO WAS EAGER TO SHOW OFF THEIR BEAUTY.

THE KITCHEN WAS FULL OF DELICIOUS SMELLS. LUCKILY FOR ME, THE COOKS WERE TOO BUSY TO NOTICE ME DIPPING MY FINGERS INTO THE POTS. BUT POLYNICES SAW ME AND INSTEAD OF SNEAKING ME FOOD, HE SHOVED ME AWAY. BEING CUPBEARER HAS MADE HIM SNOOTY. STILL HE PROMISED TO TELL ME ABOUT THE GUEST WHO DESERVED ALL THIS FUSS.

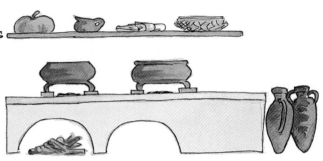

THE DOGS STARTED BARKING WILDLY AND I RAN OUT TO SEE FOR MYSELF OUR GUEST. I WANTED TO KNOW **WHO** HE WAS BEFORE POLYNICES DID!

IT WAS A FEAST FIT FOR A KING — JELLYFISH AND EGGS, SOW'S UDDERS STUFFED WITH SALTED SEA URCHINS, BRAINS COOKED WITH MILK AND EGGS, BOILED TREE FUNGI WITH PEPPERED FISH SAUCE — AND THAT WAS JUST THE FIRST COURSE! THE MAIN COURSE WAS DEER ROASTED IN ONION SAUCE, RUE, DATES, RAISINS, OIL, AND HONEY; BOILED OSTRICH WITH SWEET SAUCE; MORAY EELS WITH GOOSE LIVER; AND LOBSTER WITH ASPARAGUS.

HE ARRIVED IN A COACH, ACCOMPANIED BY A WHOLE TROOP ON HORSEBACK, SOME SLAVES, SOME NOT, AS MANY WORE THE IRON RING OF A ROMAN CITIZEN. WHOEVER WAS INSIDE WAS VERY IMPORTANT TO MERIT SO MANY ARMED GUARDS. SURELY A SENATOR, POSSIBLY EVEN A CONSUL, THE HIGHEST OFFICE IN THE STATE (EXCEPT FOR THE EMPEROR, OF COURSE).

CAVE · CANEM

BESIDES THE REAL WATCHDOGS, THE VILLA HAS THIS MOSAIC OF A DOG WITH THE WORDS "BEWARE OF DOG" IN THE ENTRY.

VEDIUS POLLIO CAME OUT TO THE CARRIAGE, WELCOMING THE GUEST HIMSELF. A SMALL MAN STEPPED OUT OF THE COACH, NOT OLD BUT NOT YOUNG, EITHER. HE WAS HANDSOME, WITH LIGHT CURLY HAIR AND PIERCINGLY CLEAR EYES, AND HE MOVED WITH THE GRACE AND ASSURANCE OF A CAT. I DID NOT KNOW THEN THAT HE WOULD BECOME ALMOST A FATHER TO ME, BUT I KNEW JUST SEEING HIM THAT I HAD MET TRUE GREATNESS.

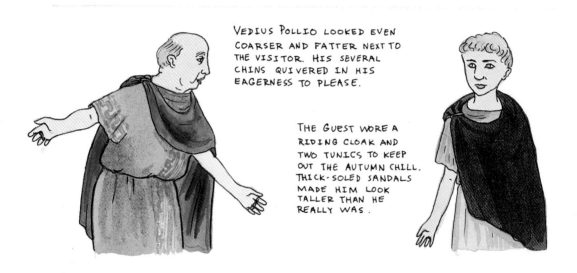

VEDIUS POLLIO LOOKED EVEN COARSER AND FATTER NEXT TO THE VISITOR. HIS SEVERAL CHINS QUIVERED IN HIS EAGERNESS TO PLEASE.

THE GUEST WORE A RIDING CLOAK AND TWO TUNICS TO KEEP OUT THE AUTUMN CHILL. THICK-SOLED SANDALS MADE HIM LOOK TALLER THAN HE REALLY WAS.

THE MAN WAS, OF COURSE, THE EMPEROR AUGUSTUS, STOPPING FOR THE NIGHT WITH US ON HIS WAY BACK TO ROME. VEDIUS POLLIO GAVE HIM A TOUR OF THE FRESHLY DECORATED VILLA, AND AFTER THEY'D RELAXED IN THE BATHS, HE INTRODUCED MY FATHER TO AUGUSTUS. FATHER HAD BEEN A FREE MAN FOR TOO LONG TO WEAR THE SERVILE MASK OF THOSE BORN TO SLAVERY. HE LOOKED THE EMPEROR IN THE FACE, PROUD OF HIS ART. AND AUGUSTUS SMILED AT HIM! HIS WIFE, LIVIA, HE SAID, WAS HAVING HER OWN VILLA NORTH OF ROME REPAINTED. PERHAPS VEDIUS POLLIO WOULD LEND MY FATHER FOR THE TASK.

VEDIUS POLLIO BEAMED, HIS FLESHY CHEEKS PLUMPED OUT EVEN MORE BY HIS SMILE. HE WAS DELIGHTED TO HAVE SOMETHING DESIRED BY THE EMPEROR AND COULD ALREADY IMAGINE HIMSELF BRAGGING THAT IT WAS HIS SLAVE WHO PAINTED LIVIA'S VILLA. WHAT A MAN OF TASTE AND DISCERNMENT HE WAS!

POLLIO SHOWED OFF HIS PAINTINGS, MOSAICS, SCULPTURES, AND GARDENS. HE WAS ESPECIALLY PROUD OF THE PONDS FOR OYSTERS AND MORAY EELS. THERE WAS EVEN AN OUTDOOR DINING AREA, SO YOU COULD WATCH THE EELS AS YOU FEASTED UPON THEM (THOUGH WHO WOULD WANT TO LOOK AT SUCH EVIL, NASTY CREATURES?). FORTUNATELY THE DAY WAS TOO COOL FOR THAT KIND OF ENTERTAINMENT.

I WAS JEALOUS OF POLYNICES HAVING THE HONOR OF SERVING THE EMPEROR. BEING A CUPBEARER HAD ALWAYS SEEMED A TRIVIAL TASK TO ME — PAINTING WAS MUCH MORE NOBLE. BUT THAT NIGHT I WANTED TO HOLD CUPS MORE THAN BRUSHES.

VEDIUS POLLIO HAD A LARGE COLLECTION OF GREEK WINE CUPS, WORKS OF ART THEMSELVES. HE WAS VERY PROUD OF THEM.

I WAS STILL A YOUNG BOY, SEVEN YEARS OLD THEN, SO THE COOKS LET ME STAY IN THE KITCHEN, WHERE POLYNICES COULD REPORT BACK TO ME WHAT HE'D SEEN AND OVERHEARD. THE ONE VIRTUE OF BEING A SLAVE IS THAT NO ONE THINKS OF YOU AS HAVING EARS, MUCH LESS A BRAIN.

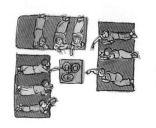

I DON'T KNOW WHO THE OTHER GUESTS WERE. NOBLEMEN, I SUPPOSE, TRAVELING WITH THE EMPEROR.

FREE MEN EAT LYING DOWN, BUT WE SLAVES SIT ON STOOLS OR THE GROUND.

AFTER POURING WINE FOR THE GUSTATIO, THE FIRST COURSE, POLYNICES CAME INTO THE KITCHEN GRINNING BROADLY.

"WHAT'S THE JOKE?" I ASKED.

"VEDIUS POLLIO LAYS OUT THIS SPREAD," SAID POLYNICES. "WELL, YOU'VE SEEN IT — TASTED IT, TOO — AND THE REGAL AUGUSTUS WON'T TOUCH IT!"

"WHAT?" I WAS AMAZED. "HE WANTS RICHER FOOD THAN THAT?" I COULDN'T IMAGINE WHAT THAT COULD BE. PEACOCK IN A PASTRY CRUST WITH HONEYED DATES?

"IT'S NOT <u>RICHER</u> HE WANTS." POLYNICES LAUGHED. "IT'S <u>PLAINER</u>! HE SAYS HE'S CONTENT WITH SIMPLE FARE. SOME EGGS AND BREAD, A BIT OF CHEESE AND OLIVES. BUT HE WANTS A GOOD WINE. I'M TO GET SOME OF THE BEST SETIAN WINE AND POUR IT INTO THE MASTER'S FAVORITE CUP!"

POLYNICES AND THE FAMOUS CUP. WE LAUGHED AS HE CARRIED IT AWAY. IT SEEMED SO FUNNY TO US—AN EMPEROR EATING LIKE A SLAVE! WE DIDN'T KNOW THAT MOMENTS LATER, IT WOULD BE THE GODS' TURN TO LAUGH AT US — AND TO TORMENT US WITH SOMETHING FAR WORSE THAN SLAVERY.

POLYNICES LEFT THE KITCHEN, AND THERE WAS SILENCE AS HE CROSSED OVER TO THE DINING ROOM. THEN THE SOUND OF A CRASH, OF SOMETHING SHATTERING, OF MY MASTER BELLOWING LIKE A MAD BULL. "POLYNICES, YOU CLUMSY OAF! YOU FILTHY IDIOT! MY BEST CUP! THE JEWEL OF MY COLLECTION!"

I KNEW WHAT MUST HAVE HAPPENED, BUT I PEEKED THROUGH THE CURTAINS, TERRIFIED. WHAT WOULD BE DONE TO MY POOR BROTHER? WOULD HE BE HUNG UPSIDE-DOWN? WOULD HE BE WHIPPED?

VEDIUS POLLIO WAS EVEN UGLIER, RED AND SWEATY WITH RAGE. HE ORDERED SLAVES TO BIND POLYNICES' HANDS. THEN HE SAID SOMETHING THAT MADE ME SHRINK INTO MYSELF WITH HORROR.

"TAKE HIM AWAY UNTIL TOMORROW," POLLIO COMMANDED, HIS VOICE HOARSE WITH ANGER. "AT DAWN HE'LL BE THROWN TO THE MORAY EELS SO I CAN ENJOY THE SIGHT OF THEM EATING HIS PRETTY FACE INCH BY INCH."

I ALMOST SCREAMED AND GAVE MYSELF AWAY. MY POOR BROTHER! AND SUCH AN UGLY WAY TO DIE! I HAD TO SAVE HIM — I HAD TO DO SOMETHING! I RAN TO FIND MY FATHER. HE COULD BEG THE MASTER TO SPARE HIS SON. IF VEDIUS POLLIO VALUED ART HE WOULD HAVE TO LISTEN. BUT I FEARED HE PRIZED HIS EELS MORE.

FATHER PALED WHEN I TOLD HIM WHAT HAD HAPPENED. "OH, GODS!" HE WAILED, "FIRST YOU TAKE MY WIFE AND NOW MY SON!"

"NO, FATHER, NOT TAKEN YET! WE MUST STOP HIM. YOU MUST STOP HIM." I WAS CRYING AND SHAKING, BUT TRYING TO SOUND STRONG AND SURE OF MYSELF, AS SURE AS A SMALL BOY CAN BE.

TOGETHER WE RAN TO THE TRICLINIUM, BUT THE SOUND OF A STERN, CALM VOICE STOPPED US FROM ENTERING. IT WAS AUGUSTUS. "YOU VALUE LIFE SO CHEAPLY THAT PAINTED CLAY IS WORTH MORE TO YOU?" HE SAID. "ARE YOU A ROMAN OR A BARBARIAN, LIKE THOSE BRUTES IN BRITANNIA WHO PAINT THEMSELVES BLUE? THE BOY WILL BE SPARED, AND I WILL TEACH YOU THE VALUE OF POTTERY."

SOMEONE THRUST POLYNICES OUT OF THE ROOM. HE STUMBLED INTO US, SOBBING—FROM RELIEF OR TERROR I COULDN'T TELL. "MY SON!" FATHER CRIED OUT, HUGGING HIM. I HELD HIM, TOO, AS TIGHT AS I COULD.

I DON'T REMEMBER MUCH OF THE REST OF THAT NIGHT. SOMEHOW I SLEPT, THOUGH I HAD TERRIBLE NIGHTMARES ABOUT MORAY EELS, WITH THEIR RAZOR TEETH AND VICIOUS EYES. IN THE MORNING WE WERE TOLD THAT AUGUSTUS HAD BOUGHT US AND WE WERE TO GO WITH HIM AT ONCE TO ROME. FATHER NEVER FINISHED PAINTING THE VILLA, AND NONE OF US EVER SAW VEDIUS POLLIO AGAIN.

MARCUS VERRIUS FLACCUS, A FREEDMAN WHO TUTORED AUGUSTUS' CHILDREN AND GRANDCHILDREN, RODE WITH US. HE ASKED FATHER ABOUT THE LEARNING POLYNICES AND I HAD HAD. I REMEMBER HE WAS VERY KIND TO US AND GAVE ME SOME FIGS TO EAT.

"SO VEDIUS POLLIO IS TRIPLY PUNISHED," HE TOLD FATHER. "HE LOSES HIS PAINTER, HE LOSES THE ENTERTAINMENT OF SEEING YOUR SON DEVOURED BY HIS NASTY PETS, AND AUGUSTUS ORDERED THAT EVERY SINGLE WINE CUP IN HIS PRECIOUS COLLECTION BE DESTROYED!" MARCUS VERRIUS CHUCKLED. "NEXT TIME HE'LL BE MORE CAREFUL WHO HE LOSES HIS TEMPER AROUND."

FATHER LAUGHED, TOO, A CREAKY, THIN LAUGH, BUT STILL A LAUGH. HEARING IT, I REALIZED IT HAD BEEN A VERY LONG TIME SINCE I HAD SEEN HIM HAPPY.

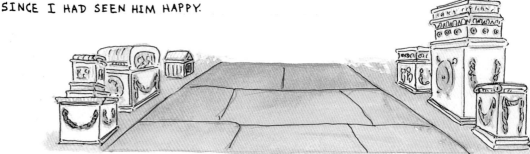

ALL I RECALL OF THAT JOURNEY TO ROME WAS THE ROAD ITSELF. THE APPIAN WAY IS A MARVEL, PAVED WITH SMOOTH STONES FITTED TIGHTLY TOGETHER AND WIDE ENOUGH FOR TWO OXCARTS TO PASS EACH OTHER.

As we got closer to the city, tombs sprouted on either side of the road. Like the Greeks, the Romans don't allow the dead to be buried within the city walls, so they line the roads leading to it instead.

It was already dark when we entered the city. Marcus Verrius explained that Augustus preferred arriving in Rome at night, so no fuss would be made by his appearance. By torchlight and the glow of the half-moon, I saw a haze of colonnades and basilicas, marble gleaming white in the dark, but I didn't see the full glory of the city until the next day.

LIVIA DRUSILLA
While other matrons dress their hair in elaborate styles, Livia wears an old-fashioned bun. Others wear fancy, colorful gowns while she wears a plain white stola. Her eyes are so sharp they slice right through you, to the bone. I can't look her in the face. I stare at her chin instead.

In the morning we met our mistress, Livia. While Augustus is the grandson of a money changer, the great-grandson of a freedman, Livia is from an old noble family, the Claudians. It was a Claudian who built the Appian Way, and many of them served as consuls in the Republic. So she has reason to be proud, and proud she is. To tell the truth, I was scared of her then — and I still am. It's said that she is the only one Augustus bends to, and I believe it.

Some women are so vain about their hair, they constantly change styles. One sculptor even carved a portrait bust with a detachable scalp so the statue could change hairdos like its mistress. Some ladies smear their hair with a grease made from rat heads, rat excrement, hellebore, and pepper. It's supposed to make their tresses beautiful, but I think it would just make them smelly!

"WHAT GOOD ARE YOU, BOY?" THOSE WERE THE FIRST WORDS I HEARD FROM LIVIA, SHARPLY SPOKEN, TOO.

"I AM LEARNING TO BE A PAINTER, MISTRESS, LIKE MY FATHER. I PREPARE HIS COLORS AND BRUSHES."

"WHAT GOOD IS THAT TO ME?" SHE SAID CURTLY.

I HAD NO ANSWER TO THAT.

"SO I THOUGHT." HER LIPS PRESSED TOGETHER AND GREW EVEN THINNER. "CAN YOU READ AND WRITE?" SHE ASKED.

"GREEK," I WHISPERED FEELING MORE AND MORE USELESS.

"NO LATIN? OF COURSE NOT!" SHE SIGHED. "ANOTHER MOUTH TO FEED, SO YOU'D BEST BE WORTH IT. WHEN YOUR FATHER HAS NO NEED OF YOU, YOU WILL STUDY HERE WITH AGRIPPA POSTUMUS AND LEARN, SO YOU CAN BE OF USE."

EVEN POLYNICES WHO IS USED TO CHARMING EVERYONE WITH HIS BEAUTY HAD NO SUCH EFFECT ON HER. "TOO PRETTY BY HALF," SHE SNAPPED. "BUT YOU'LL DO SERVING AGRIPPA POSTUMUS, SINCE HIS SLAVE DROWNED IN AN UNFORTUNATE FISHING ACCIDENT." LUCKILY FOR POLYNICES, AS CRUEL AS AGRIPPA IS TO ME, HE'S SWEET AS HONEY TO MY BROTHER.

AUGUSTUS' HOUSE IS SMALL AND SIMPLE COMPARED TO VEDIUS POLLIO'S VILLA. ATTACHED TO IT IS A MORE IMPRESSIVE OFFICIAL PALACE USED FOR PUBLIC FUNCTIONS. ON THE OTHER SIDE IS LIVIA'S HOUSE — MUCH FINER THAN AUGUSTUS', WITH MOSAIC FLOORS AND RICHLY PAINTED WALLS.

AUGUSTUS' STUDY IS HIS FAVORITE ROOM, FILLED WITH SCROLLS AND WAX TABLETS FOR NOTES. THE WALL PAINTING IS SIMPLE ARCHITECTURAL DESIGNS. THE FLOOR IS STONE, NOT MARBLE.

THOSE FIRST DAYS ARE A JUMBLE OF SMELLS AND SOUNDS AND SIGHTS. BUT I VIVIDLY RECALL RUNNING DOWN THE PALANTINE HILL WHERE THE PALACE IS TO THE FORUM. HERE IS THE HEART OF THE EMPIRE — LAW COURTS, GOVERNMENT BUILDINGS, TEMPLES, SHOPS, THE SENATE, AND, OF COURSE, THE ROSTRA, THE SPEAKER'S PLATFORM DECORATED WITH THE BEAKS OF ENEMIES' SHIPS. AT THE VERY CENTER IS THE GOLDEN MILESTONE. ALL ROADS FAN OUT FROM THERE AND ALL MEASUREMENTS ALONG THE VAST NETWORK OF IMPERIAL ROADS REFER BACK TO IT.

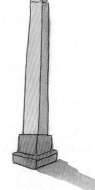

THE CITY MADE MORE OF AN IMPRESSION ON ME THAN OUR NEW HOME, I MUST CONFESS. THE BROAD MAIN STREETS HAD DRAINS FOR WATER AND MUD THAT EMPTIED INTO THE SEWERS (WHICH ALSO CARRIED OFF THE WASTE WATER FROM THE BATHS AND PUBLIC LATRINES). THE LATRINES THEMSELVES WERE A WONDER TO ME, WITH MARBLE SEATS AND STATUES, THE WASTE FLUSHED AWAY WITH A CONSTANT STREAM OF WATER, THE WHOLE THING EVEN HEATED!

THERE IS A SUNDIAL IN THE FORUM AND WATERCLOCKS IN THE BASILICAS, BUT MY FAVORITE TIMEPIECE IS IN THE CAMPUS MARTIUS WHERE AUGUSTUS SET UP AN EGYPTIAN OBELISK AS A GIANT SUNDIAL.

ANOTHER FAVORITE IS THE ARA PACIS, AUGUSTUS' ALTAR OF PEACE, ALSO IN THE CAMPUS MARTIUS. IT SHOWS A PROCESSION WITH AUGUSTUS AND HIS FAMILY, INCLUDING HIS GRANDSONS, IN MARBLE RELIEFS. FATHER SAYS IT WAS CARVED BY GREEKS AND CLEARLY INFLUENCED BY OUR PARTHENON.

BESIDES THE GRAND STREETS WITH PUBLIC BUILDINGS, I LOVE ALL THE NARROW NAMELESS ALLEYS WHERE THE REAL LIFE OF THE CITY BUSTLES — CRAMMED WITH SHOPS, GRAMMAR SCHOOLS ON THE SIDEWALKS, PEDDLERS HAWKING THEIR WARES. EVEN THOUGH CARTS AND HORSES AREN'T ALLOWED IN ROME BY DAY (EXCEPT FOR THE MANY DOING CONSTRUCTION WORK), THE STREETS ARE SO CROWDED SOMETIMES YOU HAVE TO SHOVE YOUR WAY THROUGH.

I LOVE EXPLORING THE CITY— THERE ARE PEOPLE AND GOODS HERE FROM ALL OVER THE EMPIRE — NUBIANS, SCYTHIANS, GAULS, CELTS, EGYPTIANS, JEWS, AND, OF COURSE, MANY GREEKS. AGRIPPA POSTUMUS BOASTS THAT A MILLION PEOPLE LIVE IN ROME (MOST OF THEM SLAVES LIKE ME), AND SOME DAYS I FEEL LIKE I CAN HEAR EVERY SINGLE ONE OF THEM.

SINCE I COULDN'T HAVE POLYNICES AS A COMPANION — HE WAS ALWAYS WITH AGRIPPA POSTUMUS — THE CITY ITSELF BECAME A FRIEND TO ME. UNTIL I MET MICIO. BUT THAT HAPPENS LATER. AS MARCUS VERRIUS TELLS ME, THE IMPORTANT THING TO REMEMBER WHEN YOU WRITE IS ORDER. "EVERYTHING IN ITS PROPER TIME," HE SAYS.

THERE'S NOT MUCH TO TELL OF THOSE EARLY YEARS. I WAS TOO YOUNG TO DO MUCH MORE THAN WATCH OTHERS. I WOULD HAVE PLAYED WITH AGRIPPA POSTUMUS, BUT HIS CHIEF DELIGHT HAS ALWAYS BEEN TO TORMENT OTHERS, FROM BUGS AND BIRDS TO PEOPLE, ESPECIALLY ME.

AT FIRST I FELT SORRY FOR AGRIPPA BECAUSE HE NEVER KNEW HIS FATHER. AND NOW HIS MOTHER, JULIA, AUGUSTUS' DAUGHTER, IS MARRIED TO LIVIA'S SON (FROM AN EARLIER MARRIAGE). IT'S CONFUSING.

HE'S ONLY A BOY, BUT HE WALKS AROUND WITH A PERPETUAL SCOWL.

I'M TRYING TO STUDY ROMAN HISTORY, BUT IT'S NOT EASY KEEPING NAMES STRAIGHT.

TIBERIUS CLAUDIUS — LIVIA   AUGUSTUS — SCRIBONIA

DRUSUS   TIBERIUS   JULIA   AGRIPPA
                                                    (THE GENERAL
              NO CHILD   WHO LED THE ARM
                                                    TO VICTORY MA
         GAIUS LUCIUS   AGRIPPINA   TIMES, ESPECIA
                JULIA   IN THE CIVIL W
                                                    AGAINST CLEOPA
                                                    AND MARCUS ANTO
                          AGRIPPA
                          POSTUMUS

THE CITY WAS MORE FRIENDLY THAN AGRIPPA WITH ALL ITS PARKS FOR STROLLING IN AND PORTICOS FILLED WITH ART — FRESCOES AND GREEK SCULPTURE, BEAUTIFUL STATUES BY LYSIPPAS, PRAXITELES, AND PHIDIAS. BY THE TEMPLE OF APOLLO BUILT BY AUGUSTUS NEXT TO HIS PALACE, THE COLONNADES HOUSED TWO LIBRARIES, ONE LATIN, THE OTHER GREEK. AND THE TEMPLE ITSELF HELD MORE GREEK SCULPTURE. I'VE NEVER BEEN TO ATHENS, BUT FATHER HAS, AND HE SAYS THAT THE GLORY AND BEAUTY OF ROME IS JUST AS GREAT AS THE GREEK CAPITOL'S, PARTLY BECAUSE THE BEST OF GREEK ART IS NOW HERE, PARTLY BECAUSE OF AUGUSTUS' BUILDING. HE CLAIMS TO HAVE FOUND ROME IN BRICK AND LEFT IT IN MARBLE. BUT THERE'S STILL PLENTY OF BRICK LEFT, ESPECIALLY IN NARROW ALLEYS.

BESIDES BEING A SUCCESSFUL GENERAL, AGRIPPA WAS A GREAT BUILDER, TOO. HE LEFT ROME THE PANTHEON, AN AQUADUCT, GARDENS, AND BATHS.

IN FACT, THE FIRST GLADITORIAL FIGHTS I WENT TO WERE THE FUNERAL GAMES IN HONOR OF AGRIPPA, THE FATHER OF AGRIPPA POSTUMUS. GREEK GAMES ARE ATHLETIC OR MUSICAL, BUT FATHER EXPLAINED TO ME THAT THE ANCIENT ETRUSCANS HAD MEN FIGHT TO THE DEATH BY THE GRAVESIDE OF THE NEWLY DEAD TO APPEASE THEIR SPIRITS WITH THE BLOOD OF THE LIVING. (WHICH MAKES NO SENSE TO ME BECAUSE ONCE THE BLOOD IS SPILLED, THE LIVING MAN BECOMES DEAD, TOO. SO IT'S BLOOD OF THE DEAD FOR THE DEAD.) NOWADAYS GLADITATORIAL GAMES CAN BE HELD LONG AFTER THE DEATH (AGRIPPA DIED FIVE YEARS BEFORE HIS GAMES). AND SOME GLADIATORIAL FIGHTS HAVE NOTHING TO DO WITH MOURNING, BUT ARE IN HONOR OF VICTORIES OR HOLIDAYS. THE GAMES FOR AGRIPPA WERE VERY GRAND, SINCE HE WAS SO IMPORTANT — AND BECAUSE AUGUSTUS HIMSELF PUT THEM ON. GRAND MEANT HUNDREDS OF MEN KILLED EACH OTHER AND THEY DIDN'T JUST FIGHT ONE ON ONE, BUT GROUPS AGAINST OTHER GROUPS.

MURMILLI HAVE BIG SHIELDS AND SWORDS.

THRACIANS HAVE SHORT SHIELDS AND DAGGERS.

RETIARII FIGHT WITH NETS, DAGGERS AND TRIDENTS.

THERE ARE MANY DIFFERENT KINDS OF GLADIATORS, BUT IT ALL AMOUNTS TO THE SAME THING — MEN KILLING MEN. PRIVATE BUSINESSMEN USED TO TRAIN GLADIATORS, BUT EVER SINCE THE SLAVE REVOLT LED BY SPARTACUS, A THRACIAN GLADIATOR, THE STATE CONTROLS SUCH SCHOOLS. SPARTACUS LED AN ENORMOUS ARMY OF SLAVES, DEFEATING THE ROMAN LEGIONS SENT AGAINST HIM FOR FOUR YEARS. HE WAS FINALLY BEATEN SIXTY-THREE YEARS AGO AND THE APPIAN WAY WAS LINED WITH SIX THOUSAND CRUCIFIED SLAVES. I'M GLAD I WASN'T ALIVE THEN TO SEE THAT — GLADIATOR FIGHTS ARE HORRIBLE ENOUGH.

I WAS EIGHT WHEN I FIRST WATCHED GLADIATORS. I HAD SEEN SLAVES CRUCIFIED BEFORE — SUCH SIGHTS ARE COMMON ALONG ROMAN ROADS — BUT I'D NEVER SEEN ANYTHING SO...SO...REVOLTING. I KNEW I SHOULD HAVE BEEN EXCITED AND THRILLED. THE CROWD AROUND ME CHEERED AT EACH THRUST, EACH SPRAY OF BLOOD. BUT I...I...I THREW UP. AGRIPPA SAW MY SOILED TUNIC AND PALE CHEEKS AND SNEERED THAT I WAS A DAINTY GIRL. THAT WAS WHEN HE DECIDED TO HATE ME AND MAKE MY LIFE MISERABLE, WHEN HE SAW ME AT MY WEAKEST.

I COVERED MY FACE WITH MY HANDS AND DIDN'T WATCH ANYMORE. POLYNICES KEPT A STONY FACE, THOUGH HE LATER TOLD ME HE HATED THE SPECTACLE AS MUCH AS I DID. FATHER DIDN'T GO TO THE GAMES AT ALL. HE SAID I'M GREEK, AND THAT'S WHY I HAVE NO APPETITE FOR BLOOD — I SHOULD BE PROUD OF THAT AND NOT SEE IT AS WEAKNESS. AUGUSTUS HIMSELF, HE SAID, DISLIKES THE FIGHTS AND ONLY STAGES THEM TO PLEASE THE PEOPLE. THE SPORT HE REALLY ENJOYS IS CHARIOT RACING.

THIS WRITING IS A HARD THING TO DO, PAINFUL EVEN. I DID NOT LIKE DESCRIBING VEDIUS POLLIO'S RAGE AT POLYNICES, AND I DO NOT RELISH REMEMBERING MY SHAME THAT DAY AT THE ARENA. AUGUSTUS WRITES EVERYTHING DOWN — SPEECHES BEFORE THE SENATE, EVEN SHORT REMARKS. HE SOMETIMES INVITES A CLOSE GROUP OF FRIENDS OVER TO HEAR HIM READ PROSE WORKS, POEMS, OR EPIGRAMS. HE EVEN WROTE A PLAY ABOUT THE GREEK HERO AJAX, BUT HE WASN'T PLEASED WITH IT AND BURNED IT. I'M NOT PLEASED WITH WHAT I'VE WRITTEN SO FAR, BUT I WON'T BURN IT — NOT YET I LIKE THE SKETCHES IN IT TOO MUCH. BESIDES, NOW I CAN WRITE ABOUT THE PRESENT, ABOUT ME NOW, AT AGE TWELVE, NOT ME WHEN I WAS LITTLE. THEN I WAS A RAW COUNTRY BOY, NOW I AM A CITY YOUTH.

Augustus says I write well. He says stale prose is like reheated cabbage, but my writing is crisp. I think by that he means simple. I don't change much from my first draft on the wax tablet to the finished ink on papyrus.

I still help Father, painting myself now, though he finished Livia's villa long ago. He's working on rooms for Julia now and I help paint columns and leaves. And now I can read and write Latin as easily as Greek so I'm much more useful to my mistress. I often run errands for her. I know where to buy the best papyrus, the juiciest figs, the strongest baskets. Last month she sent me to get more wax tablets for the master. I ran down the ramp from the Palatine, through the forum, down the Capitoline hill. As usual, the streets were crowded, but I'm still small enough to weave my way through.

After I got the tablets, I was in no hurry to go home. It was one of those crisp fall days like the one so long ago when I first saw Augustus. So I went to the Campus Martius hoping to find a ball game I could join in. Instead I found something much more valuable — a friend.

Some streets are so narrow, you have to walk single file down them, and the buildings are so tall — four or five floors even — they block out any sunlight. Those streets I DON'T like. I'm always afraid one of those poorly built apartment houses will collapse on top of me.

I noticed him at once. Dark and small with a pointed chin and large green eyes, he looked like a faun more than a boy. But he was definitely a boy, about my age, I guessed. What caught my eye was that he was walking on his hands.

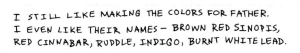

I still like making the colors for Father. I even like their names — brown red sinopis, red cinnabar, ruddle, indigo, burnt white lead.

MICIO
UPSIDE-DOWN

AND RIGHT-
SIDE-UP

"ARE YOU AN ACROBAT?" I ASKED HIM.

THE BOY LOOKED AT ME AND GRINNED. "KIND OF," HE SAID. "AND KIND OF NOT."

"IS THAT A RIDDLE?" I ASKED.

HE FLIPPED ONTO HIS FEET, DUSTED OFF HIS HANDS, AND THRUST OUT HIS CHIN PROUDLY. "I'M A CHARIOTEER," HE SAID.

"AN AURIGA? BUT YOU'RE A BOY!"

"YEP." HE GRINNED AGAIN. "START 'EM YOUNG, LIGHT, AND AGILE. THAT'S ME. I'M WITH THE GREENS. THEY'RE THE BEST TEAM, YA KNOW. WANNA SEE THE STABLE? THE HORSES ARE SOMETHING, I TELL YA!"

AND THAT'S HOW I MET MICIO, MY BEST FRIEND.

MICIO IS LUCKY. HE WILL QUICKLY EARN ENOUGH TO BUY HIS FREEDOM, WHILE I DO NOTHING TO EARN MONEY. I WISH I COULD BUY FREEDOM FOR ALL OF US, POLYNICES, FATHER, AND ME. BUT UNLESS I BECOME A BIG, TOUGH GLADIATOR AND KILL MY WAY TO A FAT PURSE, THERE'S NOT MUCH CHANCE OF THAT.

BUT CHARIOT RACING ISN'T EASY. THE REINS ARE WRAPPED TIGHTLY AROUND THE AURIGA'S BODY AND IF HE FALLS OUT OF THE CHARIOT, HE MUST GRAB THE DAGGER AT HIS SIDE AND QUICKLY CUT THROUGH THE REINS OR BE DRAGGED TO HIS DEATH. THE HARDEST PART, MICIO SAYS, IS TAKING THE TURNS. FOR THOSE YOU MUST DEPEND ON THE STRENGTH AND AGILITY OF THE OUTSIDE HORSES. THEY'RE NOT HARNESSED TO THE SHAFT LIKE THE INSIDE HORSES, SO THEY CAN SWING OUT MORE OR CUT IN CLOSER. BUT IF THEY CUT TOO CLOSE, THEY RISK CRASHING INTO THE TURNING POST. IF THEY SWING TOO WIDE, THE AURIGA COULD BE RAMMED FROM BEHIND.

MICIO SAYS HE KNOWS ONE AURIGA WHO WON MCDLXII RACES IN XXIV YEARS AND RETIRED WITH A FORTUNE OF FOUR MILLION SESTERCES!

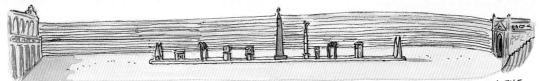

CHARIOT RACES ARE HELD IN THE CIRCUS MAXIMUS, AN ENORMOUS OVAL WITH ENOUGH ROOM IN THE STANDS FOR A QUARTER MILLION PEOPLE. SEVEN BRONZE DOLPHINS ARE TIPPED TO MARK THE LAPS, AS ARE SEVEN WOODEN EGGS. TWELVE TEAMS CAN RACE AT ONCE.

MAYBE IT'S BECAUSE BEING AN AURIGA IS SO DANGEROUS. MAYBE IT'S BECAUSE HE GREW UP IN ROME AND NOT GREECE — AFTER ALL, GREEKS KNOW THE WORLD IS ROUND, BUT ROMANS THINK IT'S FLAT! WHATEVER THE REASON, MICIO IS THE MOST SUPERSTITIOUS PERSON I'VE EVER MET. I MEAN, AUGUSTUS IS A LITTLE SUPERSTITIOUS, AGRIPPA POSTUMUS EVEN MORE SO, BUT NO ONE COMPARES TO MICIO. WHEN HE HAS A STOMACH ACHE, HE DRINKS THE WATER USED TO WASH HIS FEET — THAT WOULD GIVE ME INDIGESTION, NOT CURE IT! HE THINKS ODD NUMBERS ARE MORE POWERFUL THAN EVEN ONES (POWERFUL FOR WHAT, HE CAN'T SAY). AND HE REFUSES TO RACE WITHOUT THE GOOD LUCK CHARM HE BOUGHT FROM A WITCH. SO FAR HE HASN'T WON WITH IT, BUT HE HASN'T CRASHED, EITHER.

FATHER IS TEACHING ME LANDSCAPES NOW, SO I HAVEN'T HAD MUCH TIME FOR MICIO LATELY. BUT SOON I WILL, WHEN IT'S SATURNALIA, THE BEST PART OF THE YEAR, I THINK. EVERYONE IS IN A GOOD MOOD THEN, GIVING PRESENTS, HAVING FEASTS. AND IT'S THE ONLY TIME WHEN SLAVES CAN EAT RECLINING WHILE THEIR MASTERS SERVE THEM.

EVERYONE WEARS A FREEDMAN'S CAP DURING THE SATURNALIA — EVEN ME, EVEN THE EMPEROR! FIVE MORE DAYS AND I'LL BE FREE, AT LEAST FOR A WHILE.

I SAW POLYNICES WRITING THE OTHER DAY. I ASKED HIM IF HE'S WRITING DOWN HIS LIFE, TOO. "NOTHING SO AMBITIOUS," HE SAID, "JUST A BOOK OF SAYINGS I COPY FROM THINGS I READ. AUGUSTUS SUGGESTED I SHOULD." I FELT A PANG OF JEALOUSY. I THOUGHT THE EMPEROR ENCOURAGED ONLY ME. I'M THE ONE WHO READS SO WELL. AND I WRITE CRISPLY.

I'M NOT JEALOUS OF POLYNICES ANYMORE. FOR THE SATURNALIA, AUGUSTUS GAVE ME A ROLL OF PAPYRUS AND TWO NOTEBOOKS. POLYNICES GOT A TUNIC AND A CLOAK. I'D MUCH RATHER HAVE MY GIFTS. AND IT SHOWS THAT THE MASTER CONSIDERS ME A REAL WRITER. POLYNICES IS JUST A COPYIST.

AT THE BANQUET HE GAVE, AUGUSTUS HANDED OUT TICKETS FOR THE GUESTS TO REDEEM FOR PRIZES, ONLY THEY WERE JOKES RATHER THAN REAL GIFTS.

SOME OF POLYNICES' COPIED SAYINGS:

"SWIFTLY DONE IS BEST DONE."

"HAVE A PENNY, YOU'RE WORTH A PENNY."

"IF YOU CAN'T BEAT THE ASS, YOU BEAT THE SADDLE."

"SAVE YOUR BREATH TO COOL YOUR PORRIDGE."

"FORTUNE FAVORS THE BRAVE."

"WHAT YOU DON'T NEED IS DEAR EVEN WHEN IT'S CHEAP."

"ONLY A FOOL STUBS HIS TOE ON THE SAME ROCK TWICE."

"FORGETTING TROUBLE IS THE WAY TO CURE IT."

"WELL BEGUN, HALF DONE."

DINNER CLOTHES

THIS TICKET WASN'T FOR AN ELEGANT EVENING DRESS BUT FOR A FISH WRAPPED IN LEAVES.

I THINK THE EMPEROR ENJOYS THE SATURNALIA AS MUCH AS I DO. HE WAS HAPPY AND RELAXED, ALWAYS LAUGHING. INSTEAD OF WEARING A FORMAL TOGA AS USUAL, HE WORE A LOOSE GREEK ROBE, MUCH MORE COMFORTABLE THAN A TOGA'S COMPLICATED FOLDS.

THINGS FOR THE FORVM

THE GUEST EXPECTED A NEW WOOL TOGA, BUT GOT INSTEAD A WAX TABLET AND STYLUS.

(STILL A VALUABLE GIFT, I THOUGHT.)

LIGHTS AND LETTERS

I COULDN'T GUESS WHAT THIS COULD BE FOR. A BOOK MAYBE? IT MEANT A TORCH (THE LIGHT) AND SOME DRIED PEAS (THE LETTER "P").

THE NEXT PART OF THE DINNER I HELPED WITH. AUGUSTUS HAD SOME PAINTINGS TURNED TO THE WALL, AND THE GUESTS HAD TO BID ON THEM, SIGHT UNSEEN. SOME WERE BEAUTIFUL, DONE BY FATHER. OTHERS WERE STUDENT WORKS. (MINE, THAT IS, AND NOT TOO BAD, BUT OF COURSE NOT AS GOOD AS REAL PAINTINGS.) THE WORST ONES WERE CLUMSY MESSES—BY POLYNICES, NATURALLY. WE PEEKED FROM BEHIND A CURTAIN TO WATCH. I MAY NOT HAVE BEEN A GUEST, BUT I ENJOYED IT ALL ANYWAY.

MICIO STAYED WITH US THAT NIGHT. HE WAS GIVEN THREE DAYS FREE AND SPENT THE WHOLE TIME WITH ME. THAT WAS THE BEST GIFT OF ALL.

MICIO IN HIS FREEDMAN'S CAP

I RARELY SEE GAIUS AND LUCIUS, AGRIPPA POSTUMUS' OLDER BROTHERS, BUT THEY WERE HERE FOR THE SATURNALIA.

I'M NOT SURE WHERE THEY USUALLY ARE OR WHAT IT IS THEY DO. TRAINING TO BE EMPEROR AFTER AUGUSTUS, I GUESS, HOWEVER THAT'S DONE.

GAIUS IS THE OLDEST. HE PUT ON HIS MANLY TOGA A COUPLE OF YEARS AGO AND WAS THEN INTRODUCED TO THE SENATE. HE'S BEEN NAMED A "PRINCE OF YOUTH" AND GIVEN THE COMMAND OF A TROOP OF CAVALRY.

LUCIUS WILL PUT ON HIS MANLY TOGA THIS YEAR, PROBABLY DURING THE FEAST OF LIBERALIA. LUCKILY FOR ROME, AGRIPPA POSTUMUS' BROTHERS ARE NOTHING LIKE HIM AS MUCH AS I CAN SEE.

HAVING HIS BROTHERS AROUND BROUGHT OUT THE WORST IN AGRIPPA POSTUMUS. HE HATES THEM! ALL ROME ADORES THEM AS GOLDEN BOYS, FULL OF THE PROMISE OF THE EMPIRE, SO NATURALLY AGRIPPA IS EATEN UP WITH JEALOUSY. UNFORTUNATELY, I'M ALWAYS THE ONE HE POURS HIS VENOM ON. HE STOLE THE NOTEBOOKS HIS GRANDFATHER HAD GIVEN ME! I KNOW IT WAS HIM BECAUSE ONE WAS ALREADY WRITTEN IN AND HE TAUNTS ME BY QUOTING MY OWN WORDS BACK TO ME. I BEGGED POLYNICES TO STEAL THEM BACK FOR ME, BUT HE REFUSED.

MICIO SAID I SHOULD STEAL THEM MYSELF. I WOULD EXCEPT I DON'T RELISH THE IDEA OF A WHIPPING. I MAY BE A SLAVE, BUT I'VE NEVER BEEN BEATEN LIKE ONE. I WANT TO GROW TO BE A FREEDMAN WITH NO SCARS ON MY BACK.

POLYNICES SAID THAT IF AGRIPPA POSTUMUS CAUGHT HIM, HE'D BRAND THE LETTERS FOR THIEF ON MY BROTHER'S FOREHEAD. I SAID HIS MASTER LIKES HIM TOO MUCH TO MAR HIS PRETTY FACE, BUT POLYNICES HAS NO FAITH IN AGRIPPA POSTUMUS' AFFECTION. I REMINDED HIM OF THE SAYING "FORTUNE FAVORS THE BRAVE." AND HE REPLIED, "YES, BUT 'FOOLS DIE YOUNG' AND I'M NO FOOL."

THE OTHER THING TO DO, SAYS MICIO, IS TO PUT A CURSE ON AGRIPPA POSTUMUS. ALL I NEED TO DO IS WRITE HIS NAME ON A LEAD TABLET, PIERCE THE NAME WITH A NAIL, AND THEN PLACE THE TABLET IN A TOMB. SOMEHOW, I DON'T LIKE THE IDEA OF SNEAKING INTO A GRAVE, EVEN TO GET BACK AT AGRIPPA.

AGRIPPA

Today was the feast of Liberalia, two days past the Ides of Martius. Today Lucius became a man. The household was crazed preparing for the feast and celebration. Agrippa Postumus was more vicious than ever, sending Polynices on one ridiculous errand after another just to show how commanding he could be (for a ten-year-old). I stayed as far from him as I could to avoid his shoves and kicks, but I wanted to see the guests and what was going on. The palace was full of people. Lucius had taken off his bulla and his boy's toga marked with a purple band and wore instead the pure white toga of manhood.

A bulla is the gold charm freeborn boys wear since birth to ward off evil spells. Once a boy becomes a man, he needs no such protection.

I recognized many guests from earlier banquets. Julia, Lucius' mother, was there, of course. Her husband, however, was conspicuously absent. Tiberius is in Rhodes now, retired from public life. Rumors say he's fleeing Julia, whom he detests. He can't control her and she has more boyfriends than a hand has fingers.

Lucius looked very noble. A slave who was expert in the mysterious folds of the toga had helped him put it on. Togas are impossible to drape by yourself.

Then as quickly as it had filled, the house emptied out as everyone proceeded to the Capitoline hill to take the auspices. I felt achingly empty myself. I'm not a noble. I'm not even a freedman, but watching Lucius in that snowy white toga, I wanted nothing more than to have such a ceremony myself.

THE FEAST OF LIBERALIA IS ALSO CALLED THE FEAST OF FATHER FREEDOM. AS PART OF THE CELEBRATION, SLAVES ARE ALLOWED TO SPEAK FREELY, GRANTED A TASTE OF LIFE AS A ROMAN CITIZEN. BUT THIS YEAR IT WAS A BITTER TASTE. EVEN THOUGH OUR LEGS AREN'T SHACKLED LIKE GALLEY SLAVES, WE STILL WEAR INVISIBLE CHAINS.

FATHER CONSTANTLY REMINDS ME THAT I'M GREEK, NOT ROMAN, BUT I DESPERATELY WANT THAT MOST ROMAN OF ALL SYMBOLS, THE TOGA.

I'M HELPING FATHER PAINT NOW. AUGUSTUS LENT HIM TO LAELIUS BALBUS, WHO WAS CONSUL A FEW YEARS AGO. BALBUS BOUGHT THE HOUSE ON THE PALATINE

THAT ONCE WAS CICERO'S AND WANTS TO DECORATE IT IN A MORE MODERN FASHION THAN "STODGY, OLD CICERO" DID. FATHER SAYS I'M SKILLED ENOUGH TO TRY STILL LIFES NOW, SO I PAINTED FISH, FRUIT, AND VEGETABLES. NOT BAD. BUT NOT GOOD ENOUGH TO EARN THE FORTUNE NEEDED TO BUY OUR FREEDOM.

STILL, THERE IS SOMETHING PEACEFUL AND COMPANIONABLE ABOUT PAINTING TOGETHER, ABSORBED IN THE SHIMMER ON A FISH'S SCALE OR THE SHEEN ON A GRAPE. FATHER OFTEN SINGS OR ASKS ME TO RECITE POEMS OR SPEECHES I HAVE LEARNED. HE ENJOYS MY VOICE ALMOST AS MUCH AS AUGUSTUS DOES. BUT TODAY I WANTED TO TALK.

"FATHER," I BEGAN, "DO YOU THINK WE SHALL EVER BE FREE ROMAN CITIZENS OR WILL WE BE SLAVES ALL OUR LIVES?"

"AH, GALEN." HE SIGHED. "REMEMBER YOU HAVEN'T BEEN A SLAVE YOUR WHOLE LIFE. YOU WEREN'T BORN ONE AND I'M SURE YOU WON'T DIE ONE."

"HOW CAN YOU BE SO CERTAIN?"

"IF WE WORKED ON A FARM OR IN THE MINES — THANK THE GODS THAT WE DO NOT — WE COULD EASILY DIE SLAVES. BUT HOUSEHOLD SLAVES ALMOST ALWAYS EARN THEIR FREEDOM, WHEN THE MASTER DIES IF NOT BEFORE. I'VE SERVED THE EMPEROR WELL. HE IS PLEASED WITH MY WORK, AS IS THE MISTRESS. THOUGH YOU WOULDN'T KNOW IT FROM HER STONY FACE," HE JOKED. "BESIDES, ROME NEEDS FREEDMEN AS MUCH AS SHE NEEDS SLAVES.

SINCE NOBLES CAN'T DO ANY WORK EXCEPT LAW OR FARMING, LABOR BEING BENEATH THEIR DIGNITY, THE EMPIRE WOULD GRIND TO A HALT WITHOUT THE BUSINESS SKILLS OF THE LIKES OF US. SOME OF THE WEALTHIEST MEN IN ROME ARE FREEDMEN WHO MADE THEIR FORTUNES AS SLAVES."

"WE'RE NOT MAKING A FORTUNE," I COMPLAINED.

"NO." FATHER GENTLY SHOOK HIS HEAD, THEN SMILED RUEFULLY. "BUT WE AREN'T STARVING, EITHER. PATIENCE, MY SON. YOU WILL BE FREE ONE DAY. AND IN THE MEANTIME, AT LEAST YOU'RE MASTER OF YOUR BRUSH."

I WISH I COULD BE AS SURE AS FATHER.

SOMETIMES MICIO AND I STRETCH OUT ON THE GRASS IN THE PARK LEFT TO ROME BY MAECENAS, THE PATRON OF VIRGIL AND HORACE. WE WATCH THE CLOUDS, SMELL THE SOFT SPRING AIR, AND TALK ABOUT WHAT WE'LL DO ONCE WE'RE FREE. MICIO WANTS TO RACE STILL, BUT HE'D LIVE IN A MANSION ON THE PALATINE INSTEAD OF IN THE DORMITORY OF THE GREENS.

THREE DAYS BEFORE THE IDES OF MAY, ON A DAY OF BRILLIANT BLUE SKY AND GOLDEN SPRING LIGHT, AUGUSTUS DEDICATED HIS NEW FORUM AND THE TEMPLE OF MARS THE AVENGER. AGRIPPA POSTHUMUS, IN A GOOD MOOD FOR ONCE SINCE HE WAS GOING TO PLAY IN THE TROY GAMES, GAVE POLYNICES THE DAY OFF TO CELEBRATE ALONG WITH ALL OF ROME. EVERYONE WAS IN A CELEBRATORY SPIRIT. AUGUSTUS GAVE OUT THE GENEROUS GIFT OF SIXTY DENARII TO EACH CITIZEN AND THERE WERE SPECTACLES TO WATCH. ALONG WITH THE MONTHLY HANDOUT OF BREAD, WHAT MORE COULD A ROMAN WANT?

I DIDN'T CARE ABOUT WATCHING THE TROY GAMES. WHAT I WAS EAGER TO SEE WERE THE CHARIOT RACES. MICIO WOULD BE DRIVING A QUADRIGA, A FOUR-HORSE CHARIOT, INSTEAD OF A TWO-HORSE ONE FOR THE FIRST TIME. I WENT TO THE STABLES EARLY, AT THE FIRST HOUR OF THE DAY, TO WISH HIM LUCK.

THE STABLES WERE CRACKLING WITH NERVOUS EXCITEMENT. MICIO HAD A HARD TIME CALMING HIS TEAM. HE WAS DRIVING HIS OLD FAVORITES, WHIRLWIND AND SWEET DELIGHT, BUT HAD TWO NEW HORSES AS WELL, HAWK AND LIGHTNING. I PRAYED THE NAMES WERE AUSPICIOUS. IF MICIO WON, HE'D GET A PURSE OF SIXTY THOUSAND SESTERCES — A FORTUNE, CONSIDERING THE DAILY WAGE OF A WORKER IS ONLY TWO SESTERCES!

THERE WERE A DOZEN RACES SCHEDULED FOR THE DAY. FIRST, OF COURSE, CAME THE USUAL PROCESSION OF SINGERS, PRIESTS, INCENSE BEARERS — THE RITUAL POMP BEFORE THE FESTIVITIES. THEN CAME A FEW STUNT RACES, WITH RIDERS LEAPING FROM ONE HORSE TO ANOTHER OR SITTING BACKWARD OR MIMICKING WARFARE. LIGHT APPETIZERS BEFORE THE MAIN COURSE OF THE CHARIOTS.

EIGHT CHARIOTS WERE RACING AT ONCE, TWO FOR EACH TEAM. IF THE DRIVERS ARE SKILLED, THEY WORK TOGETHER — CLEARING THE WAY AND BLOCKING OPPONENTS, SO THAT ONE OF THE TEAM CHARIOTS WINS.

THE FOUR TEAMS ARE THE REDS, THE BLUES, THE GREENS, AND THE WHITES.

AT LAST THE REAL RACES BEGAN. I SCREAMED MYSELF HOARSE BEFORE MICIO EVEN GOT TO THE STARTING GATE. THE BLUES HAD WON TWO RACES, THE WHITES HAD WON ONE, BUT EVERYONE WAS CHEERING FOR THE GREENS. THEY'D WON TWO RACES ALREADY. I HOPED MICIO WOULD MAKE IT THREE.

I COULD SEE MICIO CLEARLY, THOUGH HE WAS THE SMALLEST AURIGA THERE. HIS TEAM WAS REARING UP, BUT THE GROOM CALMED THEM DOWN, ONLY TO HAVE THE NEIGHBORING TEAM KICK UP. FINALLY ALL THE HORSES WERE CALM — AS CALM AS COILED MUSCLES CAN BE. AUGUSTUS DROPPED THE WHITE HANDKERCHIEF, THE TRUMPET SHRILLED, AND THE HORSES BOLTED FORWARD.

AFTER THE FIRST FAR TURN, MICIO WAS LAST. THE OTHERS WERE RACING FULL-OUT, BUT HE SEEMED TO BE HOLDING HIS HORSES BACK. "LET 'EM GO! LET 'EM RUN!" I SCREAMED. BY THE FIFTH LAP, MICIO HAD EDGED UP, BUT THERE WERE STILL FOUR TEAMS AHEAD OF HIM. AND STILL I COULD TELL HE WAS HOLDING HIS HORSES BACK. ON THE SIXTH LAP, THE WHITE AURIGA WHO'D HELD THE LEAD FOR SO LONG DROPPED BACK, HIS HORSES EXHAUSTED, WITH NOTHING LEFT FOR THE FINAL LAP. AND THEN, ON THE SEVENTH AND LAST LAP, MICIO FINALLY LET HIS HORSES GO. HE LEANED FAR OVER THE CHARIOT, URGING THEM FORWARD WITH HIS BODY. THE LEADER, THE BLUE AURIGA, GLANCED OVER HIS SHOULDER AND SAW MICIO CATCHING UP AND THE OTHER GREEN AURIGA READY TO GRAB THE LEAD. DETERMINED TO WIN,

THE ARTIFIAL LAKE BUILT FOR THE FESTIVITIES WAS BIG ENOUGH TO HOLD THIRTY TRIREMES OR BIREMES AND MANY SMALLER SHIPS. IN ALL, SOME THREE THOUSAND MEN FOUGHT (NOT EVEN COUNTING THE ROWERS!).

THE BLUE AURIGA CUT THE FAR TURN TOO TIGHTLY. HIS HORSES LOST CONTROL AND PITCHED THE CHARIOT OVER. THE AURIGA CUT THE REINS AND ROLLED AWAY QUICKLY, WHILE GROOMS RAN UP TO GRAB THE WILD HORSES. MICIO'S PARTNER WAS NOW IN THE LEAD! MICIO WAS ALSO CLOSING IN, BUT BETWEEN THE TWO GREENS WAS THE OTHER BLUE AURIGA. THE BLUE CHARIOT GRABBED THE INSIDE OF THE TRACK, FORCING THE GREEN AURIGA TO TURN WIDELY AND DROP BACK. IT LOOKED LIKE THE BLUES WOULD WIN AFTER ALL. BUT MICIO'S HORSES WERE FRESH. THEY GALLOPED FULL OUT, PASSING THE BLUE TEAM IN THE LAST STRAIGHT STRETCH. MICIO WON! HE WON! I JUMPED UP AND DOWN, AS SWEATY AS IF I'D RACED MYSELF. THE CROWD ROARED LIKE A GREAT BEAST. AND AUGUSTUS PRESENTED THE PALM BRANCH OF VICTORY TO MY BEST FRIEND.

AGRIPPA POSTUMUS BOASTED THAT ALMOST THREE HUNDRED LIONS WERE KILLED THAT DAY, AS WELL AS NUMEROUS CROCODILES, HUNTED IN THE CIRCUS FLAMINIUS AFTER THE WATER FROM THE SEA BATTLE WAS DRAINED INTO IT.

THE REST OF THE DAY WAS A BLUR TO ME. AUGUSTUS HAD BUILT A LAKE TO STAGE A SEA BATTLE – THE PERSIANS AGAINST THE GREEKS. AND THERE WERE THE USUAL GLADIATORIAL FIGHTS AND ANIMAL HUNTS. BUT NOTHING WAS AS EXCITING AS MICIO'S VICTORY.

I WAS AS EXHAUSTED AS IF I WERE ONE OF THE RACEHORSES, BUT MICIO WOULDN'T LET ME GO HOME. "COME WITH ME!" HE CROWED. "AS WINNER OF TODAY'S RACE, I'VE BEEN INVITED TO A BANQUET. JULIA HERSELF WILL BE THERE."

"JULIA? THE MOTHER OF AGRIPPA POSTUMUS? AUGUSTUS' DAUGHTER?" I ASKED.

"YES!" MICIO WINKED. "THEY SAY SHE'S A CHARMING ONE WHO LOVES TO HAVE FUN. SHE'S FRIENDS WITH ALL THE BEST YOUNG PEOPLE. YOU KNOW THE KIND."

I've only heard one story about Julia (aside from Tiberius detesting her). When someone scolded her for indulging in too many luxuries, saying she should prefer simple things as her father does, she replied, "He forgets that he is an emperor, but I remember that I'm an emperor's daughter."

I didn't know, and if Julia was anything like Agrippa Postumus, I wanted nothing to do with her. But Micio insisted. He assured me that Julia is as sweet as Agrippa is sour, as light-hearted as he is lumpish. Still, how could I, a slave, go to a noble's banquet?

"I can go because I'm the victor." Micio tilted up his chin proudly. "And you can go as my slave." I laughed at the thought of being slave to a slave. (It does happen that slaves own slaves, comical though it is.) Anyway I can never resist Micio, so off we went to the dinner party.

It was held at Iullus Antonius' house, a great mansion on the Quirinal Hill. Micio seemed to know the whole complicated cast of guests. To me it was a confusing whirl of spicy perfumes, brocaded silks, pomaded hair, and rich food.

Iullus Antonius is the son of Marcus Antonius by his second wife, Fulvia. Like his famous father, he has a face women find hard to resist, but like his mother, he has a cold edge of simmering anger.

When Micio entered, everyone cheered. He was the beloved Green Auriga, the hero of the day. Iullus came up to him, clapped him soundly on the back and ushered him in. I felt like I was seeing a different Micio. Before, he'd been my friend and partner in mischief, someone I played ball with, dived with at the baths, and gambled with over knucklebones. Here he was someone else entirely, acclaimed, honored, adored. I suddenly felt shy around him, not worthy of him. We were friends by chance — here were friends he'd earned.

DICE AND KNUCKLEBONES

SILVER PEPPER SHAKER SHAPED LIKE A POMEGRANATE

SILVER CUP FULL OF PICKLED CUMIN SEEDS, A DELICACY

THE DISPLAY OF RICHES EVERYWHERE MADE ME FEEL EVEN MORE AWKWARD. AUGUSTUS DOES PREFER SIMPLICITY.

I STARED AT THE MOSAIC FLOOR DECORATED WITH ELABORATE HUNTING SCENES. I COULD
SPEAK TO THE TILED BEASTS MORE EASILY THAN TO ANY OF THE GUESTS.

I DIDN'T ENJOY THE BANQUET. I WOULD HAVE SLUNK OFF AND
GONE HOME, EXCEPT I COULDN'T BETRAY MICIO THAT WAY. I SAT ON THE FLOOR BY
HIS FEET AND DOZED OFF.

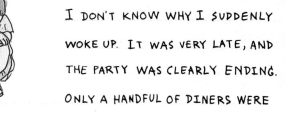

I DON'T KNOW WHY I SUDDENLY
WOKE UP. IT WAS VERY LATE, AND
THE PARTY WAS CLEARLY ENDING.
ONLY A HANDFUL OF DINERS WERE
LEFT, ALL YOUNG MEN LIKE IULLUS ANTONIUS, EXCEPT FOR JULIA — AND MICIO, WHO,
I NOTICED, WAS SOUND ASLEEP HIMSELF, UNUSED TO THE LATE HOUR AND THE WINE.

"SHOULD WE WAKE HIM UP AND SEND HIM HOME?" JULIA WAS SAYING.

IULLUS ANTONIUS LAUGHED. "HE'S EARNED HIS REST. LET HIM SLEEP,
AND HE CAN GO HOME IN THE MORNING. YOU KNOW I WON SIX THOUSAND SESTERCES
BETTING ON HIM? I ALMOST CHOSE THE OTHER GREEN AURIGA, BUT THERE WAS
SOMETHING ABOUT THIS KID . . . HE'LL BE ONE OF THE BEST, I PREDICT."

A FAT YOUNG MAN, WITH A FACE REDDENED BY WINE AND ALREADY HEAVY
WITH JOWLS, NODDED. "WE KNOW, WE KNOW. YOU'VE TOLD US A DOZEN TIMES
ALREADY. LOOK, NOW THAT EVERYONE ELSE IS GONE, LET'S GET DOWN TO BUSINESS."

JULIA GROANED. "OH, NOT TONIGHT. DO WE HAVE TO BE SERIOUS NOW?"

"YOU'LL HAVE ALL THE FUN YOU WANT AFTERWARDS, SWEETHEART, WHEN
YOU'RE MARRIED TO ME," IULLUS ANTONIUS SOOTHED. "BUT GRACCHUS IS RIGHT. WE
NEED TO ACT SOON. GAIUS AND LUCIUS HAVE BOTH REACHED MANHOOD NOW."

"WHEN, THEN?" ASKED ANOTHER MAN, WITH A LEAN, HUNGRY LOOK TO
HIS EYES, DESPITE THE HOURS SPENT FEASTING.

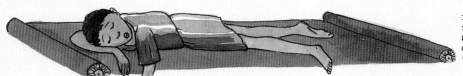

JUST THEN, MICIO BURPED LOUDLY, STIRRING IN HIS SLEEP. IULLUS
ANTONIUS LOOKED AT HIM SHARPLY.

"ENOUGH TALK FOR NOW," HE SAID. "I'VE WORKED OUT THE DETAILS
ALREADY. IT'S ALL HERE. GO HOME, STUDY THIS, AND WE'LL TALK TOMORROW." HE GAVE
EACH MAN A SMALL OIL FLASK. I DIDN'T SEE HOW THEY COULD STUDY OIL, BUT
THEY SEEMED TO UNDERSTAND WHAT HE MEANT. I WAS STILL PRETENDING TO
SLEEP, BUT I WANTED DESPERATELY TO GET HOLD OF ONE OF THOSE FLASKS.

AS THEY GOT UP TO GO, I MADE A BIG SHOW OF WAKING UP, AS IF
ROUSED BY THEIR NOISE. "MAY I GO HOME, TOO, THEN, SIR?" I ASKED IULLUS
ANTONIUS.

HE GLARED AT ME. "A SLAVE SHOULD STAY WITH HIS MASTER."

I BIT MY LIP. I NEEDED SOME EXCUSE TO GET UP. "THEN MAY I GO, ER,
WELL, TO TAKE A PISS, SIR?" I ASKED.

"GO QUIETLY AND STOP ASKING STUPID QUESTIONS!" HE SNAPPED. "WHY
DOES SUCH A PROMISING AURIGA HAVE SUCH A WOODENHEADED SLAVE?"

I MAY HAVE A WOODEN HEAD, BUT I HADN'T BEEN DRINKING ALL NIGHT.
I SET MY COURSE FOR PUDGY - THAT IS, GRACCHUS - SINCE HE LOOKED THE MOST
DRUNK. AS HE WRAPPED HIS CLOAK AROUND HIMSELF, I BUMPED INTO HIM. IT
WAS EASIER THAN I THOUGHT TO SLIP MY HAND IN HIS CLOAK AND GRAB THE OIL
FLASK. IT WAS IN MY OWN TUNIC BEFORE HE FINISHED CURSING MY CLUMSINESS.

I GOT TIRED OF STARING
INTO THE DARKNESS, SO I
LIT AN OIL LAMP AND
STARED AT THE FLAME INSTEAD.

IT WASN'T A COMFORTABLE NIGHT, TRYING TO SLEEP ON THE FLOOR
BY A SNORING MICIO. I WORRIED THAT PUDGY WOULD NOTICE THE
MISSING FLASK. BUT NO, HE WAS SO DRUNK, HE MUST HAVE FALLEN
ASLEEP AS SOON AS HE GOT HOME. STILL I COULDN'T WAIT TILL
DAYBREAK WHEN I COULD WAKE MICIO AND GET SAFELY HOME.

I KEPT THINKING ABOUT WHAT I'D OVERHEARD. JULIA WAS MARRIED TO TIBERIUS. HOW COULD SHE DIVORCE HIM AND MARRY IULLUS ANTONIUS WITHOUT HORRIBLY OFFENDING AUGUSTUS AND LIVIA? WHAT KIND OF ACTION WERE THEY PLANNING, AND WHAT DID GAIUS AND LUCIUS HAVE TO DO WITH IT? AND HOW DO YOU STUDY OIL? WHAT CAN IT TELL YOU?

MICIO WOKE UP THE NEXT DAY MISERABLE FROM HAVING EATEN AND DRUNK TOO MUCH. HE WASN'T A VICTOR, BUT A SICK WRETCH. I HELPED HIM BACK TO THE GREENS DORMITORY, THEN RACED HOME. I HAD TO STUDY SOME OIL.

THE MORNING SUN WAS A MOST WELCOME SIGHT.

ROME WAS ALREADY AWAKE AND BUSTLING AS I RAN THROUGH THE MORNING STREETS. MEN HURRIED TO CALL ON THEIR PATRONS BEFORE THE LAW COURTS OPENED, THE SINGSONG CHANTS OF SCHOOLCHILDREN RANG OUT FROM THEIR SIDEWALK CLASSROOMS, AND CARTS FULL OF BRICK AND MARBLE RUMBLED THROUGH THE STREETS.

BY THE TIME I GOT HOME, IT WAS THE SECOND HOUR OF THE DAY. CASTOR, THE DOOR SLAVE, PULLED ME INSIDE THE ATRIUM ANGRILY. "WHERE HAVE YOU BEEN?" HE YELLED. "YOUR FATHER'S WORRIED SICK, AND THE MISTRESS IS READY TO HAVE YOU DECLARED A RUNAWAY! DO YOU WANT YOUR FOREHEAD BRANDED WITH THE PERPETUAL MARK OF RUNAWAY FOR ALL TO SEE? GO TO THE MISTRESS AT ONCE AND BEG FOR FORGIVENESS!"

LIVIA IS ALWAYS FEARSOME, BUT TO FACE HER AS GUILTY AS I FELT WAS TRULY TERRIFYING. I PRACTICALLY CRAWLED INTO THE ROOM, I FELT SO LOW.

WORSE YET, AGRIPPA POSTUMUS WAS WITH HER.

"THERE'S THE DOG!" HE SNARLED WHEN HE SAW ME. "HANG HIM UPSIDE-DOWN FOR A DAY OR TWO — OR LASH HIM SOUNDLY. I'D LIKE TO SEE THE COLOR OF HIS COWARDLY BLOOD."

POLYNICES, FAITHFULLY BY HIS MASTER'S SIDE AS USUAL, PALED. "PLEASE," HE BEGGED, "FOR THE LOVE YOU BEAR TO ME, SPARE HIM!"

AGRIPPA IS UGLY ANYWAY, BUT GLOATING HE'S LOATHSOME.

AGRIPPA DID NOT LOOK AT ALL FORGIVING. HE ENJOYED TORMENTING ME TOO MUCH. BUT LIVIA, WITH HER PIERCING EYES, WAS LOOKING NOT AT ME, BUT AT HER GRANDSON. AND SHE CLEARLY DIDN'T LIKE WHAT SHE SAW.

"YOU WATCH TOO MANY GLADIATORIAL CONTESTS, AGRIPPA," SHE SAID CRISPLY. "IT IS NOT SEEMLY FOR A MEMBER OF A NOBLE FAMILY TO HAVE SUCH VULGAR TASTES. I WILL HANDLE GALEN. YOU MAY GO TO YOUR TUTOR NOW — TRY TO IMPROVE THAT MIND OF YOURS."

AGRIPPA GLARED AT ME AND, AS HE STALKED OUT, PAUSED TO KICK ME VICIOUSLY IN THE STOMACH. BUT I DIDN'T GROAN — WELL, ONLY VERY SOFTLY. GIVING HIM THE SATISFACTION OF HEARING MY PAIN WOULD HAVE HURT MORE THAN THE KICK.

I STARED AT THE FLOOR AND WAITED FOR LIVIA TO SPEAK. I WAITED AND WAITED TILL I FEARED MY BLADDER WOULD BURST. STILL, SHE SAID NOTHING

AND MORE NOTHING.

AND MORE NOTHING.

FINALLY, I CLEARED MY THROAT, VERY SOFTLY. "A-HEM."

MORE SILENCE, THEN LIVIA SHIFTED IN HER CHAIR AND SIGHED.

"YES, BOY," SHE SAID. "I KNOW YOU ARE STILL THERE." LIVIA WAS CURT, AS ALWAYS, BUT SHE DIDN'T SOUND ANGRY. STILL, WITH HER YOU NEVER KNEW. SHE'S LIKE A SPHINX — YOU CAN'T READ HER FACE.

WHAT A CONTRAST LIVIA IS TO HER STEPDAUGHTER.
JULIA WEARS LEAD POWDER TO WHITEN HER CHEEKS.
SHE IS DRAPED IN GOLD AND JEWELS AND SHIMMERING
SILKS. BUT UNADORNED AS SHE IS, LIVIA IS LIKE
A GEM STONE HERSELF — ALL SHARP EDGES AND GLITTERY
COLD. THERE'S MORE INTELLIGENCE AND WILL IN THE
ARCH OF HER EYEBROW THAN IN ALL OF JULIA.

"YOU WILL SPEND THE DAY HELPING IN THE KITCHEN. ONE OF THE SLAVES
IS SICK, AND THE COOKS NEED A HAND." LIVIA PAUSED. "I AM SURE I DO NOT
NEED TO TELL YOU THAT THIS WILL NOT HAPPEN AGAIN. THE EMPEROR HAS
FAVORED YOU TOO MUCH — I WILL NOT HAVE YOU DISAPPOINTING HIM WITH SUCH
DISRESPECTFUL, THOUGHTLESS BEHAVIOR."

  "NO, NO, MISTRESS," I MUMBLED, HORRIFIED TO THINK MY LATENESS
WOULD BE CONSIDERED AN INSULT TO AUGUSTUS, THE MAN I REVERED MORE THAN
ANY OTHER. STILL, I WAS RELIEVED TO BE PUNISHED SO LIGHTLY. MY
REMORSE WAS PUNISHMENT ENOUGH. BUT FETCHING WOOD FOR THE OVENS AND
SCRUBBING BLACKENED POTS WITH SAND MEANT THAT I HAD NO CHANCE TO
LOOK AT THE OIL IN THE FILCHED FLASK. BY DAY'S END, I'M SORRY TO SAY,
I WAS SO EXHAUSTED, I FELL ASLEEP WITHOUT EVEN THINKING
ABOUT IT.

BRONZE STOVE

I CLOSED MY EYES AND SAW YET MORE POTS TO WASH.

THAT NIGHT I HAD A STRANGE DREAM. MARCUS VERRIUS, THE
TUTOR, TOLD ME TO LOOK IN THE LIBRARY. "TO UNDERSTAND THE
OIL FLASK," HE SAID, "YOU MUST READ POMPEY." THERE WAS MORE
AFTER THAT, BUT WHEN I AWOKE ALL I RECALLED WERE THOSE WORDS.
MICIO ALWAYS SAID TO HEED DREAMS, ESPECIALLY EARLY MORNING ONES.

BRAZIER

POMPEY HAD WRITTEN A GUIDE FOR GENERALS, AND I HAD READ HIS WRITINGS MONTHS EARLIER. I TUGGED AT MY EAR, TRYING TO RECALL IF THERE HAD BEEN ANY MENTION OF OIL.

ANOTHER SILLY SUPERSTITION, I'D TEASED HIM — THOUGH ACTUALLY AUGUSTUS BELIEVES IT ALSO. AND I COULDN'T GET THE DREAM OUT OF MY HEAD. SHOULD I STUDY POMPEY AGAIN?

SOMETHING ABOUT OIL . . . I REMEMBERED! THERE'S A STORY POMPEY TELLS OF USING AN OIL FLASK TO SEND A SECRET MESSAGE. I HAD TO FIND THAT PASSAGE AND SEE HOW THE OIL WAS USED. IT WAS STILL DARK, JUST BEFORE COCKCROW, WHEN I CREPT INTO THE LIBRARY AND FOUND THE POMPEY. I READ AS QUICKLY AS I COULD, SKIMMING OVER SECTIONS, BUT THE SUN HAD RISEN BY THE TIME I FOUND WHAT I NEEDED. THERE AT LAST IT WAS:

"IT WAS AN INGENIOUS METHOD AND COMPLETELY ABOVE SUSPICION. I TOOK A PIG'S BLADDER, DRIED IT OUT, AND THEN INFLATED IT, BLOWING IT UP LIKE A BALL. WHILE IT WAS TAUT, I WROTE MY MESSAGE ON THE BLADDER, USING WAX INK TO STICK TO THE SURFACE. AFTER THE INK DRIED, I LET OUT THE AIR, INSERTED THE BLADDER INTO A COMMON FLASK, POURED IN SOME OLIVE OIL (WHICH NATURALLY FILLED UP THE BLADDER), THEN STOPPERED THE FLASK, AND SENT IT TO MY FRIEND WITH A NOTE OFFERING HIM A SAMPLE OF THE OLIVE OIL PRODUCED ON MY FARM. MY FRIEND KNEW TO POUR OUT THE OIL, BREAK OPEN THE FLASK, RETRIEVE THE BLADDER AND RE-INFLATE IT. MY MESSAGE WAS THEN EASY TO DISCOVER."

I HELD UP THE INNOCENT-LOOKING FLASK IN THE MORNING LIGHT. ALL I HAD TO DO WAS REMOVE THE NOTE INSIDE OF IT AND I WOULD UNDERSTAND WHAT IULLUS ANTONIUS WAS TALKING ABOUT. IF ONLY IT HAD BEEN SO EASY.

I SHOULD HAVE LISTENED TO MICIO — HE WAS RIGHT ABOUT DREAMS, HE MUST BE RIGHT ABOUT CURSES, TOO. FIRST CHANCE I FIND, I'M PUTTING A LEAD TABLET WITH AGRIPPA'S NAME ON IT INTO A GRAVE. THE SPIRITS OF THE DEAD MAY BE TERRIFYING, BUT <u>NOTHING</u> IS WORSE THAN AGRIPPA!

I WAS ROLLING UP THE SCROLL OF POMPEY WHEN WHO SHOULD APPEAR BUT THE DREADED AGRIPPA, EAGER STILL TO SEE ME FLOGGED, I'M SURE.

"GALEN!" HE BELLOWED. (I SWEAR, I'VE NEVER HEARD HIM SPEAK IN A NORMAL TONE.) "I THOUGHT I HEARD SOMEONE IN HERE. EAGER FOR LEARNING, EH? ALWAYS TRYING TO IMPRESS GRANDFATHER, AREN'T YOU? WELL, YOU DON'T IMPRESS <u>ME</u>!" HIS EYES FELL ON THE FLASK, AND HE SNATCHED IT UP. "WHAT'S THIS? WHY DID YOU BRING OIL WITH YOU?" HE DEMANDED.

"IN CASE MY LAMP RAN OUT," I QUICKLY ANSWERED. MY FINGERS ITCHED TO GRAB IT BACK, BUT I KNEW THAT WOULD ONLY MAKE HIM CLUTCH THE FLASK TIGHTER. I COULDN'T LET HIM KNOW HOW MUCH I WANTED IT.

AGRIPPA LIFTED UP THE LAMP. "BUT IT'S QUITE FULL. <u>VERY</u> SUSPICIOUS." HE GLARED AT ME, THEN HIS LIPS CURLED UP IN A SOUR SMILE. "I THINK <u>I'LL</u> BE KEEPING THIS." AND HE STRODE OUT OF THE ROOM — WITH THE OIL FLASK.

I COULD HARDLY BUMP INTO AGRIPPA AND STEAL THE FLASK FROM <u>HIM</u>. HE'D BE MUCH TOO WARY FOR THAT. I'D NEED POLYNICES' HELP TO GET IT BACK. THE FIRST THING TO DO WOULD BE TO TALK TO MY BROTHER — WITHOUT AGRIPPA AROUND.

IT WAS PAST THE FOURTH HOUR BEFORE I HAD MY CHANCE. I SPIED POLYNICES IN THE KITCHEN WHILE AGRIPPA WAS PLAYING DRAUGHTS WITH HIS SISTER. I DIDN'T TELL POLYNICES EVERYTHING — JUST THAT I NEEDED TO GET MY FLASK BACK, NEEDED TO KNOW WHERE IT WAS AND WHEN TO GRAB IT.

DRAUGHTS

MY BROTHER WAS EATING A LATE BREAKFAST — BREAD SOAKED IN MILK, THEN FRIED. THE SMELL REMINDED ME THAT I MYSELF HADN'T EATEN, BUT I TRIED NOT TO BE DISTRACTED. POLYNICES WAS PERPLEXED WHEN I EXPLAINED THE PROBLEM. HE COULDN'T UNDERSTAND WHY I WOULD RISK A BEATING — OR WORSE — FOR SOME OIL, WHEN I WOULDN'T DARE GET MY NOTEBOOKS AND PAPYRUS BACK. "THE OIL IS THAT IMPORTANT TO YOU?" HE ASKED. I INSISTED IT WAS. POLYNICES SIGHED. "I'LL TELL YOU THEN, BUT YOU MUST BE VERY CAREFUL. AGRIPPA LEFT THE FLASK ON THE LITTLE TABLE BY HIS BED. HE WOULD NOTICE IT MISSING AT ONCE, SO THE BEST THING TO DO IS TO TAKE IT WHILE HE'S AT THE BATHS — HE SPENDS MUCH OF THE AFTERNOON THERE. BUT ONCE HE COMES HOME, HE'LL SUSPECT YOU RIGHT AWAY. ARE YOU SURE YOU WANT TO DO THIS? YOU WON'T JUST SCRUB POTS THIS TIME."

POLYNICES WAS RIGHT, BUT I WOULD WORRY ABOUT AGRIPPA LATER. I HAD TO READ THE FLASK'S SECRET MESSAGE, NO MATTER WHAT. ONLY THE BATHS WOULDN'T OPEN UNTIL THE NINTH HOUR! THAT MEANT WAITING FIVE MORE HOURS! BUT WAIT I DID, FEARFUL ALL THE WHILE THAT BY THE TIME I READ THE BLADDER, IULLUS ANTONIUS WOULD HAVE ALREADY ACTED, AND IT WOULD BE TOO LATE TO PREVENT WHATEVER IT WAS HE PLANNED TO DO.

I WAS SUPPOSED TO GO TO THE HOUSE ON THE PALATINE AND PAINT WITH FATHER, BUT I PLEADED WITH HIM TO LET ME STAY IN OUR ROOM, SAYING I WAS TOO ILL TO BE OF MUCH USE. HE WOULDN'T HAVE BELIEVED ME IF I HADN'T LOOKED SO TERRIBLE, SICKENED BY ANXIETY AS I WAS.

THE DAY HAD NEVER PASSED SO SLOWLY — TIME SEEMED TO INCH FORWARD. FINALLY I HEARD AGRIPPA AND POLYNICES LEAVE FOR THE BATHS. I RAN STEALTHILY TO AGRIPPA'S ROOM, GRABBED THE OIL FLASK, AND WAS SOON BACK IN MY OWN ROOM WITH THE DOOR SHUT. I POURED OUT THE OIL AND CRACKED THE FLASK OPEN LIKE AN EGG. IF TIME SEEMED SLOW BEFORE, THEN

I STARED AT THE WATER CLOCK, WILLING IT TO MOVE.

SPEEDED UP AS I STOLE THE OIL, NOW IT SEEMED TO STOP COMPLETELY. AS IF IN A DREAM, I SAW THE BLADDER — JUST AS POMPEY HAD DESCRIBED IT.

AFTER WAITING SO LONG, THE ACTUAL THEFT TOOK NO TIME AT ALL — JUST A MOMENT FOR SOMETHING THAT COULD RUIN MY LIFE FOREVER.

SALVIA FOR FEVER

ROSEMARY FOR COUGHS

GARLIC TO STAY HEALTHY

I DON'T REMEMBER INFLATING IT. ALL I RECALL IS THE HORRIBLE CHILL GRIPPING ME AS I READ THE WORDS WRITTEN ON THE BLADDER. IT WAS A CONSPIRACY, A PLAN TO POISON TIBERIUS ON THE FAR-AWAY ISLAND OF RHODES. THEN IULLUS ANTONIUS WOULD MARRY JULIA AND STAND NEXT IN LINE TO RULE AFTER AUGUSTUS. ONCE THE MARRIAGE WAS CELEBRATED, AUGUSTUS, TOO, WOULD BE POISONED, LEAVING IULLUS ANTONIUS TO RULE ROME ALONE — AS HIS FATHER, MARCUS ANTONIUS, SHOULD HAVE DONE. THE DETAILS OF HOW TO KILL TIBERIUS WERE ALL DESCRIBED. EACH MAN AT THE DINNER PARTY PLAYED A PART. WHAT WOULD HAPPEN TO GAIUS AND LUCIUS, AUGUSTUS' CHOSEN HEIRS, WAS LEFT UNSAID, BUT I IMAGINED THAT THEY, TOO, WOULD BE REMOVED AS OBSTACLES.

I DON'T KNOW HOW LONG I STOOD THERE, READING AND RE-READING THOSE CURSED WORDS.

THEN THE BLADDER SEEMED TO SMOLDER IN MY FINGERS, AS IF THE RED-HOT MEANING OF THE PLOT WAS SEARING ITSELF INTO ME. I THRUST IT INTO MY TUNIC POCKET. AUGUSTUS! I HAD TO FIND HIM AND WARN HIM.

I TORE THROUGH THE HOUSE SEARCHING FOR THE EMPEROR. BUT, OF COURSE, HE WAS AT THE BATHS, TOO. HIS DOCTOR HAD PRESCRIBED COLD BATHS FOR HIM, AND HE FOLLOWED THE REGIME RELIGIOUSLY. IF IT WAS AGONY WAITING FOR AGRIPPA TO LEAVE SO I COULD SNATCH THE FLASK, IT WAS EVEN WORSE WAITING FOR AUGUSTUS TO RETURN NOW THAT I KNEW WHAT HORRIBLE SECRETS IT CONTAINED.

I KEPT THINKING OF JULIA'S PRETTY FACE. DID SHE KNOW THAT HER BOYFRIEND WAS PLOTTING TO KILL HER HUSBAND, FATHER, AND SONS?

IT WAS LIKE I WAS LOOKING AT THE EVIL FACE OF TREASON AND MURDER.

IF JULIA TOOK PART IN THE PLAN TO KILL HER FATHER, ROMAN JUSTICE WOULD EXACT A TERRIBLE PENALTY. THOSE GUILTY OF PARRICIDE ARE STRIPPED, PUBLICALLY FLOGGED, THEN SEWN INTO A SACK WITH A ROOSTER, A SNAKE, A DOG, AND A MONKEY (EACH ANIMAL SYMBOLIZES A VICE). BLEEDING AMONG THE FRANTIC BEASTS, THE CRIMINAL IS THROWN INTO THE TIBER RIVER.

THE SUN WAS LOW IN THE SKY BEFORE I SAW MY CHANCE. I KICKED THE DOOR OF THE STUDY POLITELY. "ENTER," CALLED AUGUSTUS. THE DOOR SLAVE LET ME IN. "GALEN." AUGUSTUS FROWNED WHEN HE SAW ME. "I HEAR FROM AGRIPPA POSTUMUS THAT YOUR BEHAVIOR HAS BEEN TROUBLING."

"YES, MASTER, BUT PLEASE ALLOW ME TO SPEAK," I BEGGED.

"I DO NOT NEED TO HEAR EXCUSES." AUGUSTUS FINGERED THE PAPYRUS SCROLLS HEAPED ON THE TABLE. "I AM SURE YOU UNDERSTAND IF I HAVE MORE IMPORTANT MATTERS TO TEND TO. BESIDES, LIVIA HAS PUNISHED YOU, AND I AM ALWAYS CONTENT WITH HER DECISIONS."

"MASTER, IT'S NOT THAT," I SAID DESPERATELY. "IT'S SOMETHING ELSE—SOMETHING URGENT FOR ONLY YOU TO KNOW ABOUT."

THAT WAS AS FAR AS I GOT BEFORE THAT PLAGUE AGRIPPA BROKE INTO THE ROOM.

"THERE THE VILLAIN IS!" HE YELLED TRIUMPHANTLY, POINTING AT ME. "THE THIEF! GRANDFATHER, HE ROBBED A FLASK FROM MY ROOM!"

AUGUSTUS LOOKED AT ME STERNLY. "DID YOU ENTER AGRIPPA'S ROOM AND TAKE SOMETHING?"

"HE CAN'T DENY IT!" AGRIPPA SNAPPED.

"CAN YOU?" PRESSED AUGUSTUS.

I SHOOK MY HEAD. "NO," I SAID HOARSELY.

I COULDN'T BEAR TO READ THE DISAPPOINTMENT IN AUGUSTUS' FACE. HE THOUGHT I'D BETRAYED HIM, GIVEN HIM POOR THANKS FOR ALL HIS KIND ATTENTIONS.

AGRIPPA GRINNED GLEEFULLY. "I SHOULD CHOOSE THE PUNISHMENT, SHOULDN'T I, GRANDFATHER? I'M THE ONE HE WRONGED, SO IT'S UP TO ME, RIGHT?"

"YES," SAID AUGUSTUS COLDLY AND DELIBERATELY. THE TONE OF VOICE ALONE WAS LIKE A WHIP ON MY BACK. "IT IS UP TO YOU, AGRIPPA. BUT I EXPECT YOU TO BE JUST — AND COMPASSIONATE."

"I'LL BE MORE THAN THAT, I'LL BE KIND!" DECLARED AGRIPPA. "I COULD HAVE HIM THROWN TO THE WILD BEASTS." HE PAUSED, RELISHING THE THOUGHT. "BUT I WON'T. I'LL BE SATISFIED WITH A BRANDING. LET HIM WEAR THE SIGN OF THE THIEF FOR THE REST OF HIS LIFE!"

AUGUSTUS SIGHED. "GALEN IS YOUNG. IT SEEMS HARSH TO SCAR HIM OVER SUCH A SMALL THEFT."

AGRIPPA EXPLODED, "YOU SAID IT WAS MY CHOICE! BUT NOTHING IS REALLY MINE. MY FATHER'S LANDS, HIS FARMS, HIS RICHES — THEY SHOULD BE MINE. I'M THE SON! BUT YOU, YOU STEAL EVERYTHING FROM ME — EVEN JUSTICE!"

I COULD HEAR AUGUSTUS CLENCHING HIS TEETH. PLEASE, I THOUGHT, PLEASE DON'T GIVE IN TO A BRAT'S TANTRUM. BUT AUGUSTUS TURNED HIS FACE AWAY, LOOKING OUT THE WINDOW TO AVOID MY PLEADING EYES.

"SO BE IT, AGRIPPA," HE SPAT OUT THE WORDS. "YOUR CHOICE IT IS."

AGRIPPA PRACTICALLY DANCED OUT OF THE ROOM. HE DIDN'T EVEN NEED TO KICK ME.

"MASTER," I SAID SOFTLY.

"I DO NOT WANT YOUR EXCUSES." AUGUSTUS TURNED AWAY FROM ME. "I FAVORED YOU, EDUCATED YOU WITH MY OWN FAMILY, AND HERE IS HOW YOU REPAY MY TRUST. AND OVER SUCH A TRIFLE, GALEN! I MISJUDGED YOU TERRIBLY. I THOUGHT I SAW TALENT AND A HUNGER TO LEARN. BUT I WAS WRONG." HE WALKED TO THE DOOR.

I couldn't let him go. I had to warn him — he HAD to listen.

"Master, I beg you, hear me!" I spoke quickly, rushing to get the words out before he cut me off. "It's NOT about the theft. I have something else to tell you — something VERY important."

"No games, Galen," he said. "I have no patience for them."

"It's NOT a game! It's about Julia!"

"Julia?" Augustus' manner changed entirely. He turned to look at me expectantly.

I explained in a torrent of words, anxious to get it all out— the banquet, the oil, the plot. Augustus stood like a stone the whole time I spoke. When I was finished, he held out his hand sadly and I placed the bladder in it for him to read himself. When he finally spoke, it was as if the words cut his mouth to say them.

"My daughter... my only child... blood of my blood. I was warned. Spies told me of her wild behavior, the bad company she keeps. But this... this goes beyond..." He walked stiffly out of the room, his eyes

hollow with anguish. I felt horrible. I wish I did not have to break his heart to save his life.

AUGUSTUS WENT TO THE SENATE THE VERY NEXT DAY, REVEALED THE CONSPIRACY, AND ORDERED THE ARREST OF THE FIVE MEN INVOLVED. JULIA HE SENTENCED TO EXILE ON AN ISLAND, PANDATERIA, FAR FROM THE EXCITING CITY SHE LOVED. NO MORE BANQUETS OR PARTIES FOR HER. NO MORE BOYFRIENDS, EITHER. NO MEN WERE ALLOWED TO BE NEAR HER — NOT EVEN SLAVES. THE SENATORS BEGGED HIM NOT TO BE SO HARSH TO HER, BUT AUGUSTUS SAID THAT IF THEY HAD WIVES OR DAUGHTERS LIKE JULIA, THEY WOULD THINK HIM JUST.

IULLUS ANTONIUS WAS SENTENCED TO DEATH, BUT THE OTHERS ONLY EXILED. LIVIA WAS ESPECIALLY FEARFUL TO SEE IN THOSE DAYS — SHE WAS LIKE A LIONESS ROUSED TO PROTECT HER CUBS. I WAS TERRIFIED SHE WOULD NOTICE ME IN THE TURMOIL OF THE PALACE AND REMEMBER THAT I WAS TO BE BRANDED, SO I STAYED OUT OF SIGHT AS BEST I COULD.

IT WAS AS IF AUGUSTUS SHUT JULIA OUT OF HIS HEART AS WELL AS OUT OF ROME. "WATER AND FIRE WILL MIX BEFORE SHE RETURNS TO ROME," HE SAID.

AGRIPPA POSTUMUS WAS NOT SO EASY TO AVOID, BUT RIGHT AFTER HIS MOTHER'S PUNISHMENT, HE DIDN'T DARE PRESS FOR MINE. INSTEAD, HE TAUNTED ME. "I WON'T FORGET, GALEN." HE SNEERED. "YOU'RE STILL A THIEF AND YOU WILL BE BRANDED. JUST WAIT AND SEE."

THE DAYS WHEN MICIO AND I HAD DREAMED OF FREEDOM SEEMED FAR AWAY. NOW I JUST HAD NIGHTMARES OF LETTERS SEARED INTO MY SKIN.
MICIO URGED ME TO RUN AWAY. "YOU'RE GOING TO BE BRANDED ANYWAY," HE ARGUED. "WHY NOT RISK IT? I'LL HIDE YOU IN THE STABLES."
BUT EVEN HE KNEW THAT WOULDN'T WORK. IT WOULD BE A FEW DAYS AT BEST BEFORE I'D BE DISCOVERED.

TEN DAYS AFTER JULIA'S EXILE, THE PALACE WAS NO LONGER AS TENSE. THINGS ALMOST FELT NORMAL. AGRIPPA POSTUMUS SENSED IT, TOO, BECAUSE THAT DAY WHEN I CAME HOME WITH FATHER AFTER A DAY OF PAINTING, HE WAS WAITING FOR ME. POLYNICES, BY HIS SIDE, LOOKED MISERABLE.

"TOMORROW," SAID AGRIPPA (AND, FOR ONCE, HE DIDN'T YELL— HE MUST TRULY HAVE BEEN HAPPY), "YOU WILL NOT GO PAINTING. TOMORROW YOU WILL STAY HERE, SO I CAN BRAND YOU MYSELF." HE SMILED AND LOOKED EVEN UGLIER.

THEN A HAND CAME DOWN FIRMLY ON HIS SHOULDER. "NO," SAID A VOICE. IT WAS AUGUSTUS! "NO," HE REPEATED CALMLY. "GALEN TOOK ONLY WHAT YOU HAD FIRST TAKEN FROM HIM. AND MORE THAN THAT, HE HAS DONE ME A GREAT SERVICE. HE HAS SAVED MY LIFE, THE LIFE OF MY STEPSON,

AND THE PEACE OF THE EMPIRE. NO, FAR FROM BEING BRANDED, TOMORROW HE SHALL BE FREED."

I LIFTED UP MY HEAD AND LOOKED AUGUSTUS IN THE EYES — SOMETHING I HADN'T BEEN ABLE TO DO SINCE THAT AWFUL DAY IN HIS STUDY. FREED? I COULDN'T BELIEVE IT. FREED?

"MY FATHER?" I WHISPERED. THE WORDS CAUGHT IN MY THROAT. "MY BROTHER?"

"ALL OF YOU." AUGUSTUS SMILED.

FATHER HUGGED ME TIGHTLY, AND POLYNICES HELD ME, TOO. ALL OF US— FREE, FREE!

THAT NIGHT POLYNICES AND I WERE TOO EXCITED TO SLEEP. INSTEAD, WE WENT OUT TO THE GARDEN, LOOKING AT THE STARS AND FEELING PART OF A MUCH BIGGER WORLD THAN JUST A DAY BEFORE. RIGHT BEFORE HE YAWNED AND FINALLY FELL ASLEEP, POLYNICES SAID, "YOU KNOW THE BEST PART OF BEING FREED? I'LL NEVER HAVE TO SEE AGRIPPA'S UGLY FACE AGAIN!" AND JUST AS SWEET, I THOUGHT, WAS THE SIGHT OF AGRIPPA'S FACE TWISTED WITH DISAPPOINTMENT, RAGE, AND HUMILIATION — IT WAS AS IF HE'D BEEN BRANDED INSTEAD OF ME.

EARLY THE NEXT MORNING, AUGUSTUS HIMSELF TOOK US TO THE HOUSE OF LIBERTY, NOT FAR FROM THE CAPITOLINE, WHERE THE CENSOR'S OFFICE IS. FATHER'S NAME WAS INSCRIBED AS A FREE CITIZEN OF ROME, WITH POLYNICES AND I LISTED AS HIS FREE SONS, TO BECOME CITIZENS, TOO, WHEN WE BECAME MEN.

MY FATHER LAUGHED, SEEING HIMSELF WEARING A TOGA AND A CITIZEN'S IRON RING. HE'D ALWAYS THOUGHT OF HIMSELF AS A GREEK, AND HERE HE WAS, TRULY A ROMAN NOW.

AND WHEN I TOLD MICIO OUR GOOD NEWS, HE JUMPED AND CHEERED THE WAY I HAD WHEN HE WON HIS RACE. WHEN HE FINALLY STOPPED JUMPING, I HUGGED HIM AND WHISPERED IN HIS EAR, "AND IT'S ALL THANKS TO YOU — YOU AND THAT BORING BANQUET!"

So now Father has his own workshop in the Carinae district, with our home above it. He's become a popular portrait painter, especially of senators. Polynices tends the farm north of Rome that Augustus gave us, and me, I paint, too, mostly walls of houses still. I like having more space to work with. Right now I'm decorating the house Micio bought. He earned his freedom a year after I gained my own.

Best of all, next month for Liberalia, Polynices will put on his manly toga. And I'll be there to help him drape it. I need to start practicing now so when my turn comes, I'll get the crisp, dignified folds just perfect.

OUR SHOP, WITH THE SIGN I PAINTED FOR IT

Author's Note

WRITING AUTOBIOGRAPHIES, SKETCHES, LONG LETTERS, AND SPEECHES WAS COMMON ROMAN PRACTICE, BUT UNFORTUNATELY FEW OF THE MORE PERSONAL DOCUMENTS HAVE SURVIVED. THERE'S NO KNOWN BOOK LIKE GALEN'S, AND THE AUTOBIOGRAPHY AUGUSTUS WROTE IS NOW LOST. BUT READING CICERO, PLINY, CATULLUS, MARTIAL, OVID, AND PETRONIUS (TO NAME JUST A FEW) NOT ONLY GETS US CLOSER TO DAILY LIFE, BUT TO THE TONE SUCH WRITINGS WOULD TAKE.

I CHOSE TO USE CONTRACTIONS TO CONVEY THE ROUGH INFORMALITY OF EVERYDAY SPEECH. WHILE HISTORIES AND SPEECHES ARE USUALLY TRANSLATED WITHOUT CONTRACTIONS, MORE INTIMATE WORKS LIKE LETTERS, EPIGRAMS, AND POETRY CONSISTENTLY HAVE CONTRACTIONS. FAR FROM STUFFY, THE ROMANS WERE OFTEN COARSE — WRITING A WHOLE POEM, FOR EXAMPLE, ACCUSING A DINNER GUEST OF STUFFING HIS NAPKIN WITH TIDBITS TO TAKE HOME ON THE SLY. IN FACT, THE ROMANS WERE TO THE GREEKS WHAT THE AMERICANS WERE TO THE FRENCH IN THE 19TH CENTURY. AFTER ALL, THIS IS A CULTURE WHERE ONE OF THE MOST FAMOUS ORATORS, CICERO, GOT HIS NAME FROM AN ANCESTOR WHO HAD A NOSE LIKE AN OVERGROWN BEAN — CICERO MEANS "BIG CHICKPEA!"

THE CHARACTERS IN THIS BOOK ARE ALL REAL, EXCEPT FOR GALEN, HIS FAMILY, MICIO, AND THE DOOR SLAVE, CASTOR. EVERYONE ELSE REALLY EXISTED, AND THE STORIES TOLD ABOUT THEM ARE HISTORICALLY ACCURATE — FROM THE ONE ABOUT VEDIUS POLLIO, AUGUSTUS, AND THE UNNAMED SLAVE BOY CONDEMNED TO DEATH FOR HIS CLUMSINESS BUT REPRIEVED BY THE EMPEROR, TO THE STORY OF JULIA'S TREACHERY AND EXILE. AGRIPPA POSTUMUS WAS AS NASTY AS GALEN DESCRIBES. AUGUSTUS EVENTUALLY EXILED HIM TO AN ISLAND BECAUSE OF HIS BRUTISH RAGES, AND THE FIRST THING TIBERIUS DID UPON BECOMING EMPEROR WAS TO HAVE HIS STEPSON KILLED.

RESEARCHING THIS BOOK, I READ EVERYTHING I COULD FIND FROM THE LATE REPUBLICAN PERIOD TO THE EARLY EMPIRE AND AM ESPECIALLY INDEBTED TO THE HISTORIANS SUETONIUS, DIO CASSIUS, TACITUS, AND PLUTARCH. PLINY THE ELDER'S NATURAL HISTORY PROVIDED DETAILS ABOUT PAINTING AND PIGMENTS. AS THE ROMANS DID BY JO-ANN SHELTON WAS AN INVALUABLE SOURCEBOOK OF OTHERWISE UNPUBLISHED DOCUMENTS — FROM ELECTION GRAFFITI ON THE WALLS OF POMPEY TO CURSES PLACED ON RIVAL CHARIOTEERS. STEVEN SAYLOR'S SERIES OF ANCIENT ROMAN MYSTERIES PROVIDED A LIVELY SENSE OF THE ANCIENT CITY AS WELL AS THE IDEA FOR A SECRET MESSAGE CONVEYED IN AN INNOCENT-LOOKING OIL FLASK. WHEN I CALLED THE AUTHOR OUT OF THE BLUE TO ASK PERMISSION TO USE THE FLASK, HE NOT ONLY GENEROUSLY AGREED BUT GAVE ME THE NAME OF THE ORIGINAL ANCIENT SOURCE. I'M GRATEFUL, TOO, TO NATALIE KAMPEN, CLASSICIST AT BARNARD, FOR HER CAREFUL READING OF MY MESSY MANUSCRIPT. WITH HER HELP, I AVOIDED INACCURACIES AND ANACHRONISMS. BUT THE BIGGEST RESOURCE OF ALL WAS THE CITY OF ROME ITSELF. BEYOND THE MUSEUMS, CATALOGS, AND HISTORICAL SITES, TRACES OF ANCIENT ROME ARE EVERYWHERE, GIVING A SENSE OF THE AMAZING CITY IT WAS. I WAS LUCKY TO HAVE SPENT THE YEAR WRITING THIS BOOK THERE, SEEING AUGUSTUS' HOUSE ON THE PALATINE, THE PAINTINGS FROM LIVIA'S VILLA NORTH OF ROME, THE TOMBS ALONG THE APPIAN WAY, AND MUCH MORE, ALL OF WHICH WOULD HAVE BEEN PART OF GALEN'S WORLD — AND BECAME PART OF MINE.

Some Clarifications for the Modern Reader

Galen wrote his book in the year 2 B.C., but since the use of dating from the birth of Christ wasn't introduced until much later (in the 4th century A.D., under Constantine), he would call it the year 752 ab urbe condita (that is, from the founding of the city, Rome). The calendar we use, however, is basically Roman, developed by Julius Caesar to make the months consistent with a solar rotation.

The day was divided into twelve hours, with the first starting at dawn—so the third hour would be eight o'clock or nine o'clock, depending on the time of year. Night was similarly divided into twelve hours, but the days would have longer hours in the summer and shorter ones in the winter, so an hour was a flexible notion of time.

To make this book easier to follow, I've included the letters J and K, not in the Latin (and therefore Roman) alphabet. I've also written the letter U the way we do now, not as a V as the Romans would have.

Slavery in the ancient world differed greatly from our modern notion of it. It was widespread, and being a slave was not a question of race, but of fate. Prisoners of war, people captured by pirates, babies left exposed to die—all could become slaves. Slaves who worked in the mines, on farms, and in the galleys of ships had hard lives and little prospect of liberation. Slaves, however, were not allowed to serve in the army or navy, so movies such as BEN HUR, where slaves are chained to the oars of a military ship, are inaccurate, as is the more recent film, GLADIATOR. By the early empire, slaves could not be forced to fight in the arena. Gladiators were condemned criminals, prisoners of war, or men choosing to risk their lives for a chance at fame and fortune.

Household slaves had much easier lives and were often freed. Greek slaves in particular were highly valued as skilled and educated, the kind of slave who could expect to be freed. Unlike African slaves in the American South, Roman slaves were allowed to earn and keep their own money (slaves could and did own their own slaves) and to use their money to buy their own freedom. Slaves were allowed a form of marriage and such unions were recognized in that families would not be split up, although children born to slaves would themselves belong to the master.

Since all work other than law and farming was considered beneath the dignity of a Roman senator, slaves and freedmen — men once slaves, but then freed, as distinct from free men who have never been slaves— made up the bulk of the empire's middle class. Slaves would act as business partners of noble Romans, running their affairs. Once freed, the slaves (now freedmen) continued to operate their own businesses. Imperial slaves — slaves working for the emperor— had tremendous power in the daily running of the state, becoming a strong civil service and, as individuals, becoming some of the wealthiest and most influential Romans.

By the second century A.D., four years after Galen's book was written, many Romans had slave blood, so high was the rate of intermarriage, and ex-slaves made up the bulk of citizens. It was a society with room for many people like Galen and his family.